Sweetbriars

Leaving The City

Hollie Anne Marsh

www.sweetbriarsfarm.com

Sweetbriars
Leaving The City
A novel by Hollie Anne Marsh
Copyright © 2018 by Hollie Anne Marsh

Cover photograph by Paul Ruffle Photography.
Cover photograph courtesy of the Heppelthwaite family, with Faye Heppelthwaite and the pony Gigman Boy George.
Cover design by Rick Holland at Vision Press.
Edited by Anna Bowles.

ISBN: 978-8409017348

For José and Lucas

Chapter 1

The Sullivan family pulled up at the heavy wooden gates of the farm. "Sweetbriars" read the name on the gate, and there was a large "For Sale" sign planted out the front.

The farm was set in the English countryside of Dalesea, just over three hours from bustling London. When the Sullivans had received an inheritance, they had looked at a few properties for sale, but none seemed as promising as Sweetbriars. Or, to quote the estate agent... "you *have* to come see it, straight away, as it will not, I repeat, will not, stay on the market long."

Looking out the car window, Cate released a breath she hadn't realised she'd been holding. This place might make all her dreams come true, or it might be the end of everything she'd ever known and loved.

Cate shifted in her seat. Her sore muscles reminded her of her riding lesson the evening before – her very last one with Bridget. She couldn't imagine not seeing her trainer anymore. Bridget wasn't just a riding instructor – she was Cate's friend and confidante.

Sweetbriars was a far cry from the family house in Hattersfield that Cate had lived in all her life, with its familiar nooks, crannies, and quirks. Even though Cate loved the idea of having her horses at home, three hours was a long way from her best friend Beth and Bridget.

Yet here they were.

As the family drove towards the house, wooden fences lined both sides of the driveway, framing fields of long grass. The previous owners had been living overseas and had sold their horses.

Cate spotted stables on the left. They were wooden and shaped like an L, facing a garden patch full of weeds. On the right-hand side, set further back from the drive, was a two-storey soft grey stone house whose large rectangular windows were adorned with wooden shutters painted a faded green. There was a large red front door with ivy growing ornately around it. Beside the white, pebbled path was a freshly-mowed lawn like thick green carpet.

Her father, stopped the car, and Alex, her older brother, jumped straight out, eyeing the stables.

"Cate, shall we take a look?" Alex asked, his eyes wide with excitement, as she slammed her car door shut.

Cate readily agreed, and they looked at their parents, Sarah and David, for consent.

"Well, we are fifteen minutes early to meet the estate agent," said Dad, looking at his watch and then down the driveway.

"I think it should be OK... the estate agent said we could look around if we got here first," added their Mum. "But please stay out of trouble and don't open anything that's closed – or go where you shouldn't go! We'll meet you at the house when you're finished."

There were twenty stables! They were surrounded by a reddish-coloured brick path that felt soft when you walked on it. Cate realised it was purpose-made for horses to walk on so they couldn't slip.

Next Cate found herself in a spacious room that could be used as a social area. It had a kitchenette, table and chairs, a comfy old green sofa, a log-heater, and a large window overlooking a dressage arena. Nestled in the corner of the room was a small bathroom with a shower and toilet.

Cate plopped down on the sofa to test it out. "It's pretty comfy, Alex," she said, as she sank into the sofa, then disappeared in a poof of dust, "Eww, now I'm covered with dust!"

"Well, it wasn't going to be clean, was it, if the stables have been empty for so long?" asked Alex, shaking his head and laughing.

Cate lifted herself carefully off the sofa to try to prevent more dust going into the air, and brushed herself off.

Next door was a tack room. There were racks and hooks for storing saddles and bridles on one wall, with a long metal bar fixed to the other wall to hang horse blankets on. Beside the tack room was a room for storing horse feed, with large metal silos on the walls. There was also an elevated loft area for hay storage.

The stables felt kind of lonely without horses or equipment, but it wasn't hard to imagine how great they would be with horses living there.

Alex had got ahead of Cate during their inspection, and she hurried to see what he had discovered. As she left the stables, she spotted a wash bay. There were two stalls, separated by a metal bar, and hot and cold-water taps on the wall. Cate was glued to the spot for a moment picturing herself pampering her beloved palomino show horse, Odette, in there.

When Cate caught up with Alex, he was walking around the riding arena checking the surface with the toe of his boot, mimicking their dad. Dad did this to check the quality of the sand, as a poor quality surface can damage a horse's legs.

"It's something special, isn't it?" Cate admitted to her brother when she got within speaking distance. Alex looked up and nodded with a thoughtful look on his face.

"I wonder where the show-jumping paddock is, though," he said, furrowing his eyebrows. "I'm sure Mum said there was another arena to set up show-jumps."

"Maybe it's on the other side of the stables?" wondered Cate as she looked beyond the stable block.

As they walked around to the other side of the stables, they could see a fenced square arena with silver jump wings standing upright. Upon closer inspection, they spotted faded show-jumping poles beside the jump wings, hiding in tufts of green grass and sand. Cate and Alex leant over against the fence, surveying the second arena.

"Wow... two arenas and so much space," said Alex as he ran his fingers back and forth over the smooth wood, in awe of what they had seen.

"I know!" cried Cate. "Can you imagine what fun Mickey will have here? He can run to his heart's content." Mickey was the family dog – a spotty Jack Russell with ginger eyebrows and floppy ears. Full of mischief and boundless energy as all terriers are.

"And there are jumps here already!" continued Alex. "We can paint them, and make them look like new."

Alex's phone beeped and he took it out of his pocket. "It's Mum and Dad. They want us to join them at the house."

"OK, let's go," said Cate. After seeing the stables, she really hoped the house wouldn't turn out to be a disappointment.

They walked across the driveway to meet their parents at the front of the house. The estate agent offered to show them around, but Alex and Cate preferred to do their own house tour, and she agreed.

The house was bigger than their home in Hattersfield, with large windows that let in a lot of light. As well as having five bedrooms, it had two living areas, and many of the rooms overlooked the garden and fields where the horses could be turned out. There were two large bathrooms, one downstairs and another upstairs. In the living area there was a large stone fireplace. It was right in the middle of the house, and made it feel warm and cosy.

The kitchen had oak décor, and there was a solid wood dining table with matching chairs set in the middle of the room. Large glass doors opened out from the kitchen, overlooking the back garden. Alex and Cate opened the doors to find a large patio made of bricks.

The garden was neglected with soil beds beside the fences, and overgrown plants mixed with weeds. At the back of the fence line, in the middle, was a square metal gate, leading to the horse fields. When they poked their head over the gate, they could see the fields nicely sequenced into neat squares. It reminded Cate of a jigsaw puzzle.

When they joined their parents in the kitchen, Alex said, "I bags the bedroom with the attic trapdoor."

Cate chimed in, "I'd like the bedroom beside the bathroom." She was thinking about their old house, where there was only one bathroom, a floor away from Cate's room.

"Kids, you're getting a bit ahead of yourselves," said their Dad, grinning.

Mum's eyes lit up as she said, "What we could do with the gardens here... and there's even an AGA oven."

Dad gave them a resigned look and crossed his arms. "OK, OK, I get the hint. You guys are a *little* bit interested in moving here, right?" Dad's eyes twinkled. "Now, most importantly, your Mum and I must see these stables."

They left the house and found the estate agent leaning on her car, speaking on her phone. As she saw them approach, she finished her call.

"Do you have any more questions?" she asked in a polite, professional tone.

"No, I think we're good for now. We'd like to look at the stables, and it seems the kids know the way," said Cate's Mum, letting out a small laugh.

"OK, well, I'll be here at the car if you need anything," replied the agent.

They thanked her and began the tour with Alex and Cate leading the way. Cate excitedly pointed out the dressage arena, social area, and wash bays. Alex pointed out how light and airy the stables were, and, of course, the purpose-built show-jumping arena.

In Hattersfield, their livery yard had only one arena and there had been disputes over the show-jumps being left out – meaning they had to be set up and put away each time. At Sweetbriars, they could leave the jumps up, which would save a lot of time. As the arena was square, they could also leave a course of show-jumps up to replicate a competition.

Finally, the family walked around the rest of the property. The fields were much larger than the ones they were used to with dewy knee-high grass and sloped downhill a little, facing a valley. The fences were post and rail, made of solid wood, and some of the fields were divided with old English hedges, some that were over six feet tall.

As Cate was looking towards the back of the field, a dark shape near the back fence caught her attention. She squinted and thought she saw some-one pushing a bike along, then second-guessed herself as it was shady and getting dark. Cate wondered if she should mention it to her family, but as quick as she had seen it, the figure was gone.

Chapter 2

The negotiating was done, and the family was leaving Hattersfield in eight weeks' time. Finally, they could move to the 'real' English countryside and set up the equestrian centre they had wished for.

Mum and Dad had been complaining more often about Hattersfield getting busier with traffic and new construction. They also complained about the rising cost of maintaining many horses, even on DIY – driving to their stable every morning and night to look after their horses – without paying anyone to help.

The Sullivan family had eight horses, including a chestnut mare called Copper and a young bay horse called Bliss. Mum, was training them both for show-jumping. Alex had Fritz – a giant grey Holsteiner who also jumped. Cate's Dad had Bear, who was mainly a bit of a plod, and Cate had her golden palomino, part Warmblood, Odette, that she competed in horse shows with. There were three other horses that weren't ridden. Maggie the broodmare and her babies, Flute and Jambo, who would be ridden one day when they were older.

Mum and Dad had met through horse-riding many years ago. Mum was a riding instructor and mainly taught show-jumping, both at their stable and Pony Club. They had talked about moving to the countryside for years, but it was only a year ago, when Mum received an inheritance, that it had become a possibility.

Most of the time Cate liked being a Sullivan. She loved horses and going to the stables every day. But this came with responsibilities such as mucking out and grooming, even on the grimmest, muddiest days. Mum had very high standards, both for caring for the horses and riding them. Cate felt like Alex had more freedom than she did since he was getting older and had study commitments. Lately, he was beyond forgetful about horse-related things and sometimes skipped evening feed times. This meant Cate or her Mum had to fill in for Alex, feeding and putting blankets on Fritz. Cate didn't really mind as she was fond of Fritz, but she felt that if *she* missed a day at the stable, her Mum wouldn't be as forgiving. Alex was also absent-minded. He left things in random places, like brushes or sweat scrapers, and despite Cate chiding him about being tidy, it didn't seem to make a jot of difference.

Cate couldn't stop thinking about how much she would miss Beth and Bridget. She remembered how Beth had sobbed when Cate told her she was moving to Dalesea. Beth´s Mum had promised that Beth could get the train to Dalesea on weekends or during the school holidays, but it wouldn't be the same as being around the corner from each other. Bridget, however, was thrilled for

Cate, and promised her they would see each other at shows and keep in touch.

It would be a big change for the whole family, with Mum leaving her loyal horse-riding clients and Dad leaving his London accountancy firm. Alex had mixed feelings about leaving his friends and school, but on the other hand, he wanted to take riding more seriously at their own farm.

For each of the Sullivans there were things they would miss in Hattersfield, but having their own farm they could call home was a dream come true.

The weekend before they moved, Cate arranged a sleepover at Beth's house. They planned to watch a movie on Netflix.

Beth lived fifteen minutes away in an area where the houses were modern, architecturally designed, and all unique. Cate loved Beth's shiny house full of gadgets. It was the opposite of Cate's simple brick house, full of old 'hand me down' furniture that had many stories and memories attached to it.

The girls ate popcorn and watched a film on Beth's mammoth flat-screen TV. Cate was trying not to be solemn, but it was hard to believe that she would soon be so far away from her best friend.

Cate and Beth had known each other since kindergarten and never fought. Beth was liked by *everybody* at school, both students and teachers. She was tall, with olive skin, long dark wavy hair, and hazel eyes which she inherited from her Spanish mother. She looked a lot different than Cate who had shoulder length blonde hair and bright green eyes. Cate was only of average height and sometimes wished she could have some of Beth's features, like her long legs! Cate could talk to Beth about *anything*. They both knew each other's secrets, and if they were sad or unsure of something, one was always able to help the other to feel better.

When the movie came to an end, the girls were stretched out on the sofa in their usual positions, their heads touching in the corner where the sofa sections met.

Beth turned towards Cate and said, "I am so going to miss you, Cate." Tears pooled in her eyes. "I am sorry – crying again!" Then she gave a small laugh and wiped her eyes. "I know *I will* see you, but not every day. We won't be able to ride together in the forest. We won't be able to go to Pony Club together and laugh at Mr. Pike." Mr. Pike taught riding to music at the Pony Club. They sometimes did impersonations of the 'oh-so serious Mr. Pike' that put them in hysterics. "We won't be able to go shopping for new jodhpurs or saddle cloths anymore… and the list goes on."

Cate felt a lump forming in her throat, and she fought back tears. She put on a brave face and hugged Beth's shoulders. "I know... but you can come up to our new farm *anytime*, and we can go exploring in the forest. We'll be buying more horses for Mum to give lessons on, so you'll always have a horse to ride. I'll come back and visit, and we can talk and message all the time, so we'll be totally up-to-date," said Cate as consolingly as possible.

"Sure, I know," Beth said after a minute or so, her bottom lip quivering. "But it won't be the same."

"It will be different... but we'll have lots of new adventures to share with each other," said Cate brightly.

"That's true," agreed Beth, forcing a smile.

The next morning, Cate had breakfast with Beth and her parents in their shiny kitchen. Beth's Mum, Margarita, made fluffy scrambled eggs on toast with freshly-squeezed orange juice. There was a funny feeling in the air today, and the girls' natural chatty behaviour was subdued. Margarita seemed more cheerful than usual, livening up breakfast with tales of when she was a teenager and used to go horse riding at her cousin's farm near Dalesea. Cate suspected this was making things worse for Beth, as not only was her best friend leaving, she was going to the countryside to have adventures without her!

When Cate got home she heard her Mum calling from the study.

"How was the sleepover?"

Cate walked through mostly bare rooms and leant against the doorframe of the study. Her Mum was sitting at the desk, concentrating on some papers, and looked up.

Cate swallowed, then said, "Good... although I'm really going to miss Beth. I'm not sure I want to move away!" Cate cried, as she crossed her arms and blinked back tears.

Mum took her glasses off, rubbing her eyes. She leaned back and said, "That will pass with time, Cate. You'll meet new friends, and Beth will still be around sometimes – so you'll have even more friends." She paused and then continued, "You kids haven't had many changes growing up, but as you get older you need to get used to them. When people you love stop being in your life it can feel like the worst thing in the world, but then other good people come along, and you realise that the change was for the best."

Cate felt lighter somehow. "Thanks Mum. I'm sure you're right. I guess it'll just take time, like you said."

"You'll be so busy helping us set up the new farm that you won't have time to be sad about Beth. OK?"

"Sure, Mum," Cate replied, as she uncrossed her arms and smiled.

"Now, Cate, we need to check every room and make sure we haven't forgotten anything. Then get ready for the farewell party, OK?"

"OK," replied Cate, already distracted from Beth. She had to find some clothes to wear to the party! Most of her things were already packed, so it wouldn't be easy to find something suitable.

"I think you forgot to leave some un-horsey clothes out," said Mum. "Fortunately I remembered..." She smiled as she held up Cate's favourite winter outfit, a silver, sparkly v-necked sweater that went over black tights.

"Oh, Mum, thanks for pulling that out!" replied Cate. "I would have had *no* idea where to find the right clothes."

"Yes, I know! I am your Mum. Luckily I've had twelve years of knowing you, and how you *sometimes* forget things if they aren't horse-related."

Later that evening, Cate decided to say farewell to the horses at their DIY stable. Cate knew most of the horses well – their stories, ailments, and quirks. The stables were next to the Honeypot Pub where the farewell party would take place.

Cate gave each and every horse a kiss on the nose and a Polo mint. When she arrived at Odette's stable, she opened the door and was greeted with a nudge from Odette's soft velvet nose. Cate found solace in Odette's soft mane and couldn't hold back her tears.

She realised she needed to let out the tears she had been holding back these past days, but after a few minutes she calmed down. Cate dried the part of Odette's mane that was wet with tears with her sleeve and whispered she was sorry for being dramatic. Odette looked at Cate with kind, enquiring eyes, and Cate dug a Polo mint from her pocket and gave it to her.

As Cate was closing the stable door, she could see her riding instructor Bridget approaching. Bridget checked on the horses at dusk every night.

"Cate darling, what are you doing out here? Everyone is waiting for you inside."

"I was just checking on Odette," Cate stammered. She hoped it wasn't obvious she had been crying.

Bridget studied Cate's eyes for a moment, and then linked her arm through Cate's.

"Darling, let's go enjoy this party. Everyone is here to see you off to your incredible new adventure. We are going to have a terrific time!"

All the Sullivans' friends were in the pub.

It was surreal. Cate felt like she was watching the scene from a distance. She managed to say the right things and perform the right actions, and casual conversation masked her disbelief that they were actually leaving. It made her look at the old pub in a new light – she wouldn't get to see the owner Eddie and his wife Julia on a Sunday any more. She wouldn't be able to eat their famous pies.

Beth stayed by Cate's side all night as they chatted with their friends. Cate told her what she knew about Sweetbriars, and then the usual conversation followed about life in Hattersfield. People made plans to meet at Pony Club on Saturday to practise for the inter-zone competition; they made plans for a cross-country day... and the list went on. Cate found it was reassuring to have Beth at her side, and between them they made sure that any reference to the future included each other... "When you come to Sweetbriars," "When you come to stay for the weekend in Hattersfield."

As a farewell gift, their friends gave the Sullivans a brass plate saying, 'Home is where the horses are.' They loved it, as those words were finally going to come true! Mum said she already knew where she would hang it – above the door to the tea room, as she called the social area.

That evening – the last evening in her childhood home – Cate tried to fall asleep. She was exhausted, but her mind was racing with the day's activity as she anticipated the big move. As she had done many times before, she traced the engraved letters of the friendship bracelet she wore until she got sleepy. *Cate and Beth, best friends forever.*

She pushed the bracelet inside her pyjama sleeve, keeping it close to her skin, grateful for having had such a special friend for so many years.

Chapter 3

The Sullivans moved to their new house on a frosty Friday morning in late winter. They'd spent four weeks packing up their old home and hired movers to help with the furniture. Mum and Dad had taken most of the horse equipment to their new farm the weekend before, so they were able to fit all the horses into the old lorry for the final trip.

The drive to Dalesea was full of anticipation and tinged with melancholy. With last night's stable farewell party fresh in their minds, the family was unusually quiet the first half of the journey. Stopping for lunch, about an hour away from Dalesea, they saw the countryside was more spectacular than ever with lush, rolling fields dotted with horses of every colour and size. Practical questions and comments turned into livelier chatter as they got closer to the farm.

Once they'd pulled into their new driveway and opened the heavy wooden gates, the family excitedly descended on the stables. They unloaded the horses carefully, putting them into clean stables with soft straw so they could safely survey their new surroundings. All the horses behaved well, apart from Maggie, who hadn't left her field much in years. Now she strutted around her stable with her tail held high, nostrils flaring, whinnying out to the other horses.

Once the horses were settled with food and warm blankets, the Sullivans began the task of settling into their new house. The movers had been given a list so they could put the furniture in the right rooms, and the family unpacked the things they needed for their first night. Cate's father drove to the closest village and bought take-away fish and chips. They ate ravenously in their new kitchen, all hungry and exhausted from the move. That night Cate was so tired she didn't feel her head hit the pillow.

The following morning, Cate woke up early in her unfamiliar bedroom. At the crack of dawn she heard strange sounds, but after a few minutes she fell back into a deep sleep. She woke again at around seven o'clock when her alarm went off. Such a short, deep sleep had made her fuzzy-headed, but she quickly came to and sprang from her bed. She dressed swiftly, eager to eat breakfast, and most of all, to see the horses just outside the house!

Cate joined her parents in the kitchen, gobbled down some toast, and then went out to meet her brother in the stables. Alex had given the horses breakfast and started mucking out. He had put a few of the horses in the closest fields so the family could keep an eye on them while they got used to their new surroundings.

Cate walked towards Odette's stable with a carrot in her pocket. As the mare heard her footsteps she poked her head out and rapped her front legs eagerly on the stable door. Cate patted her nose and slipped the carrot out. Odette ate it in a few polite bites and looked towards the fields. It was time for Odette to join the other horses outside.

Cate changed her stable blanket for a waterproof one and led Odette into the field. Once Odette was safely inside and the gate was shut, she nibbled tentatively at the long grass, keeping one ear flicked forward and the other one back, as she eyed her new surroundings. She started to paw one of her front hooves against the ground and sniffed the grass curiously. Cate unclipped the lead rope and stroked her golden neck.

"Off you go, girl, enjoy the grass – you deserve it," said Cate to the mare.

Alex's horse, Fritz, whinnied to Odette, and she raised her head, pricked her ears, and floated across the field at a trot to meet him. They touched noses briefly over the fence, and after a loud snort, Odette turned and galloped around the field, ears still pricked and tail held high. Fritz tried to join her, cantering up and down the fence line, bucking here and there. After a few circles, Odette stilled and stood looking into the distance. After a few more minutes, she lowered her muzzle and started to graze. Fritz followed her lead, snatching at the long grass but staying as close to Odette as the fence would permit.

After the horses settled, Cate decided to go into the house and start unpacking her things.

In her own bedroom, Cate didn't know where to start. She sat on her bed and suddenly a sense of loss washed over her. Her spacious new room felt cold with bare walls and large brown moving boxes stacked by the door.

She leant back, resting her head against the wall, and closed her eyes. She was thinking about her old Pony Club and how there was a rally day this weekend.

One sad thought led to another. All her old horse plans were scuppered.

She sighed loudly and as usual, her mother's voice came into her head... she knew her Mum would tell her about all the wonderful new competitions she could enter in their new county... but Cate didn't want to think about that right now. She wanted to be right back where she was before, where she'd felt at home.

After a few moments she forced her eyes open and looked out the window. She could see Odette and the other horses grazing from her window. Cate sat there for what seemed like an eternity, simply watching.

Her phone beeped, and she could see she had messages from Beth and Bridget checking to see she'd settled in OK. Cate stood up and took a photo with her phone, showing the view from the window, and sent it to them both.

The messages made her feel better, and after a few hours she had made some progress unpacking things and even put her favourite posters up. She was surprised at how much cosier her room felt compared to only hours before.

After lunch Cate put on her jodhpurs and boots and fetched Odette from the field. The weather had improved with the sun poking through the clouds.

She led Odette to the stables and joined Alex, who was preparing Fritz to be ridden. Fritz whinnied to Odette as they rounded the corner, and Cate tied Odette up in the stall beside him. Odette gave Fritz a cool look of acknowledgement, but then kept a pleased eye on Cate as she massaged her soft shiny coat with a body brush. Cate then cleaned and oiled her hooves and untangled her mane and tail. She put protective boots on all four legs and then finished her preparation by spraying Odette's mane and tail with a glossy spray, until it was smooth and silky.

"Cate, do you want to ride in the arena with me for half an hour, and then go explore the bridle paths out the back?" Alex asked.

"Sounds like a plan," Cate replied enthusiastically.

Cate and Alex led their horses to the new arena where Cate got onto the mounting block beside the gate and slid softly into her dressage saddle, putting the balls of her feet carefully into the stirrup irons. She patted Odette's neck, then asked her to walk forward. The mare responded, flicking her hooves into a rhythmic walk. She stretched her silky neck out and pricked her ears forward as she took in the new arena. She only spooked once – at an old pot plant, beside the letter C at the top of the arena.

To warm Odette up, Cate trotted and cantered her around the arena until she started to relax, softening her back and neck into a more comfortable position.

Fritz was excitedly rushing around the arena in a bold, energetic trot. Alex had asked him to do a few transitions, changing from walk, to trot, and then to canter, getting the gelding to focus and trot in an even rhythm.

"Are you ready to go exploring?" Cate called to Alex across the arena.

"Yep, Fritz feels a bit calmer, finally!" Even though Alex was a confident rider, he wanted to make sure Fritz was as quiet as possible. He was a big horse to control, standing at seventeen hands high, and he could be quite a handful if he was scared or excited outside the farm.

They left the arena and proceeded up the path to the back of their farm. As they passed fields with long grass, skittish rabbits ducked on and off the path in front of them. One rabbit ran right under Fritz's front legs and the big gelding got a fright, leaping over the rabbit. Alex stayed seated and patted him, laughing at the horse's behaviour.

Odette primly stepped aside to give Fritz more space.

"I knew he'd take fright at something – although I thought it might happen *after* we left the farm," said Alex, rolling his eyes and smiling.

"Well, it's all part of his jump training," replied Cate with a giggle.

When they arrived at the hedge that bounded the back of the property, Cate leant over Odette to open the gate. They turned out of the farm onto a country lane with a dirt road and fields on both sides. They had been told this was the best way of reaching the main entry to the bridle paths.

After a few minutes, they saw a small cream-coloured wooden house on their left-hand side. Whoever lived there must be the Sullivans' closest neighbour from behind the farm. The house had a small front garden and an old picket fence, splotched with cracked green paint. There were dense bushes overflowing onto the pathway that led to the front door.

The house paint was also weathered. The window-shutters were rickety, and some of the wood looked rotten.

But one patch of grass beside the overgrown path was carefully trimmed and stood in contrast to the rest of the house. Beside the building was a small covered space where a little white car stuck out its nose. On the sides of the house, a couple of windows were boarded up, giving the impression that the property was vacant.

There were empty fields on both sides, with wire fencing strung up using random tree trunks as posts. The house looked uncared for, apart from the manicured patch of lawn.

"I wonder who lives there?" said Cate.

"It looks empty to me – you can see the car's covered in dust. And those bushes would make it difficult to walk up the front path," said Alex.

"Maybe the people are old and can't look after the gardens very well any more. Or perhaps they don't need to use the rooms where the windows are boarded up?" Cate added, shrugging her shoulders.

Once past the house, they got to the bridle paths and discussed which way to go. They agreed to take the path directly in front of them as it appeared to lead into the heart of the forest. The trail was wide and clear with sodden leaves providing a squelchy, mulch-like surface.

It was still winter and many of the trees were barren, but the forest looked inviting anyway. Large English oaks lined the paths, and there was dense woodland as far as the eye could see.

After the horses settled into a rhythmic walk and the path was drier, they asked their horses to trot. After five minutes, they followed a turn in the path and were suddenly blinded by a brilliant winter sun as the trees cleared, revealing open fields with hundreds of sluggish-looking woolly sheep. The horses hesitated at the unfamiliar sight, slowing their pace, but resumed normal speed once they adjusted to the light. Then they ducked back into dense forest, and the light dimmed again. As they rounded another corner, the horses' necks lifted, and they hesitated with Odette dropping into a walk. Fritz followed Odette's lead and closed in behind her shoulder, letting the older mare lead.

They heard voices, and soon three people came into view.

They were a woman and a man, who looked around Cate's parents' ages, and a petite young girl. As they approached, Cate realised the girl was closer to her age than she'd first thought. The family was bundled in dark, heavy winter clothing, wearing gloves and hats in spite of the mild late winter temperature. The woman and girl wore heavy black-rimmed glasses and had similar coloured vivid red hair. The man had ghost-like pale skin and grey hair poking out from his woolly winter cap.

"Hello there," Alex called out politely.

The man looked surprised to see the horses as the soft ground had masked the usual clip-clop sound of hooves. He paused and dug his hands deep into his pockets as he said, "Hello. Nice day for a ride." His lips tightened into a smile, revealing small uneven teeth.

"Yes, it is," said Cate and Alex almost in unison.

The woman made eye contact, then cast her gaze down at the leaves under her feet, seeming to wait for a cue from the man. He looked straight ahead as if to end the conversation, and Alex and

Cate carefully walked the horses around the three figures. Cate could see the girl's eyes were glued to Odette.

When they were out of earshot, Alex and Cate started to talk about the encounter.

"What a strange family. The lady and the girl didn't say a word, and they were dressed for Arctic conditions," said Cate.

"Yes, they seem a bit awkward. I suppose that must be their daughter with the same red hair as the lady," replied Alex.

"I wonder if they live around here?" said Cate.

"Well, I guess we'll find out soon enough," replied Alex.

"Should we canter the horses?" asked Cate, as she spotted a stretch of open trail ahead of them.

"OK, go on then," replied Alex encouragingly. Cate put her outside leg behind the girth and asked Odette to canter. She bounded into canter, with Fritz following suit and the horses' strides somehow matched well for speed. Fritz's large and now relaxed steps fell into the same rhythm as Odette's bouncy canter stride.

They let the horses go a bit more, lightening their seats and leaning forward. Both Cate and Alex relaxed and enjoyed the feeling of freedom.

After five minutes or so, they had to bring the horses back to a walk and decide whether to keep on going straight or turn left. They decided to take a chance on turning left, hoping the path might make a circle and take them home. They were in luck, and after half an hour they found themselves back on the road where they had started.

Almost home now, they passed the old wooden house again and saw the man from their earlier encounter in the forest. He was opening the gate and had the dusty white car idling, ready to go somewhere. Mystery solved – the three strangers were the Sullivans' closest neighbours!

The man gave his strange smile again and waved briefly, then put his hat on, pulling the front down over his eyes. He quickly got into the car and appeared to fiddle with the radio, a stony look of concentration on his face.

Alex glanced at Cate, raising an eyebrow. Cate responded with a puzzled smile as they made their way home.

Chapter 4

Cate woke easily with the spring sunshine streaming through the windows and the birds singing. She felt butterflies in her stomach as she remembered this was the first day at her new school.

Her alarm clock said it was six, but she didn't have to get up until six thirty, so she lay in bed for a while, thinking. They had been living at Sweetbriars for over a month, but it didn't feel like more than a week!

She decided to get up and give the horses their morning feed. As it was spring, it didn't take too long to finish the morning chores, as the horses didn't need blankets or their stables cleaned. They lived out in the paddocks in spring and summer.

Cate entered the room where they stored the horses' fodder and picked up Odette's food bucket, which had been prepared the night before. As she did this, she felt a small whoosh of air and a tickling sensation down her arm. She screamed and dropped the bucket as she watched a brown mouse scamper away, darting into a hole in the corner of the wall. She stood there shaking, almost wondering if she had imagined it, it happened so quickly.

Luckily the horses' buckets had covers so their food couldn't be contaminated, but with the warmer weather coming, one mouse could turn into many – as Cate had learned at her previous stables. She walked around the stable, loudly stamping her feet so as not to have another run-in and planned to tell Mum and Dad when she saw them.

Cate continued picking up the horses' buckets and went to put food in the containers hanging on the gates. As she did this, she started to hatch a plan.

When she went back into the house her parents were eating breakfast.

"Mum, Dad, guess what happened to me?" Cate announced loudly.

"What happened, dear?" said her father as he put down his newspaper and looked at Cate with concern.

"Well, there's a big, brown mouse living in the feed room. He just jumped on me when I picked up a feed bucket, and ran down my arm," Cate said, grimacing. She took a deep breath, waiting for her parents' response. When there'd been a mouse infestation at the old stables, the owner had introduced two cats and the mice disappeared pronto. Cate was anticipating and hoping for a similar situation. She was already picturing a cute little kitten.

"Oh no, I hate mice," her Mum said. She sighed and looked at Dad.

"We can lay some traps or get a pest control company in. Where there's one mouse, there're usually many more. Things will only get worse with this warm weather," replied Dad calmly, and he turned his attention back to reading the newspaper.

Cate took a deep breath, then said, "I have an idea. We could get a cat, or even a kitten. Do you remember at our old stable the mice disappeared almost instantly after they brought in cats?"

Cate's parents looked at each other, pausing in thought.

"We could even get a rescue cat from the cat home..." Cate suggested, to sweeten the idea.

"Cate, I think that's a wonderful idea," remarked Mum, looking at Dad for agreement.

Dad put his paper down and crossed his arms. "Hmm, yes, I can't see why not... I suppose all good stables need a stable cat," he said with a glint in his eye and a grin spreading across his face.

Cate suspected her parents had said yes so easily because they knew she'd been feeling a little down after the move. Pleased at the prospect of getting a cute kitten, Cate forgot about first-day school nerves and decided to get dressed for the day.

Her new school uniform included a navy knee-length skirt, a white shirt, and a navy jumper or blazer, although that was only for autumn and winter. The blazer pocket was embossed with the school emblem, and its name – Dalesea College. Pupils also had to have white socks, (or black tights in winter), which Cate would wear with her new Mary Jane patent leather shoes her mum had bought her in London.

Cate was glad she had a uniform, so she didn't need to think about what to wear!

As for her hair, she spent at least twenty minutes fiddling with it. Eventually, Cate decided on a plain old ponytail as nothing else looked right. She added purple crystals studs in her ears – at least part of her outfit would have a little personality!

They arrived at school and dropped Alex at the seniors' entrance. It was their second visit, and once again Cate was astonished at how much space there was. They walked up a tree-lined path to arrive at an old cream-coloured building with a sign saying 'General Enquiries.'

A lady who looked to be in her fifties was sitting behind the main desk, talking on the phone.

She had short, spiky dyed-blonde hair that stood up at least five centimetres off her head and wore yellow plastic-framed glasses, a dark purple v-necked top, and jeans. Cate thought she looked quite trendy.

"I'll be with you in a jiffy," said the woman with a wide smile, removing her phone earpiece.

After a few minutes, she finished her call and introduced herself as Mrs. Magill. She asked for Cate's name and entered it into the computer. Then she fished a folder out of a box with Cate's name written neatly on the front. It was an enrollment pack, which Mrs. Magill said contained everything Cate would need to know to manage her first days at the Junior School.

Mrs. Magill marked out the important locations on a school map and explained the school timetable. Cate's first class would be Mathematics with Miss Dixon in classroom 4C.

"There's nothing like getting stuck into a bit of algebra to calm first-day school nerves, right?" joked Mrs. Magill as she winked at Cate.

"Sure," said Cate, giving a polite smile. She was looking forward to the distraction of schoolwork to do exactly that!

"Well, I think that's everything," said Mrs. Magill, standing up. "If you need anything, please come and see me." She beamed, then looked beyond them to a girl with long hair sitting with a man who Cate guessed was her father. Cate had been so engrossed with Mrs. Magill that she hadn't heard them enter the office.

As they left the office, Cate could hear Mrs. Magill ask the girl her name and whether she was there to enroll. The girl said she was new and her name was Violet. Cate hoped she would be in her class so she wouldn't be the only new girl.

Mum gave her a goodbye kiss and promised to come back and collect her after school.

Cate felt nervous as she walked through a series of tree-lined paths, consulting her map and taking in the buildings around her. They were also cream-coloured with floor-to-ceiling windows revealing individual classrooms. Cate found 4C written above a door; she paused and swallowed, and then took a deep breath. The room looked slightly chaotic, with noisy girls in clusters dotted around. Cate couldn't see a teacher.

She entered the room quietly, taking small steps towards what must be the teacher's desk, then waited awkwardly, taking in her surroundings. Her mouth felt dry and her palms sweaty, but she did her best to feign a confident look as she leant against the table. There were around twenty girls in the room, many curiously eyeing Cate. She was playing with a loose strand of hair and looking in her new school diary when Miss Dixon entered.

The teacher took centre stage beside Cate at her desk. Now Cate felt even more awkward with all the students staring at the two of them. She wasn't sure where to stand.

After saying good morning to the classroom, Miss Dixon turned to Cate and said crisply, "You must be one of my new students. What is your name?"

"It's Catelyn... or Cate as most people call me," Cate said, trying to keep her voice steady.

The door swung open and banged against the wall as the tall girl from the office entered the room. All eyes swiveled towards her.

"Ah, and you must be my other new student?" asked Miss Dixon.

"Yes, I'm Violet," the girl replied with a clear, even voice and an easy smile. She glided towards Miss Dixon and Cate.

"Wonderful," Miss Dixon replied. "I'll seat you together at the empty desk in the second row." She gestured to the desk.

The girls greeted each other with polite *hellos*. Violet had cornflower-blue eyes and glossy strawberry blonde hair half-tied back with a blue silk ribbon. The way she carried herself made her seem taller than she actually was. Cate felt childish by comparison.

They organised their things on the desks for the class. Violet was meticulous, lining up her pens (red, blue, *and* black), two pencils, and a ruler with precision.

Miss Dixon asked the students to introduce themselves. By the end of the introductions Cate had already forgotten every student's name except for Violet's.

Cate thought Miss Dixon was beautiful with long blonde hair tied into a simple ponytail and light green eyes fringed with long dark eyelashes.

She was patient and explained things carefully in a clear voice. She regularly asked if everyone understood an exercise before moving on to the next, and the lesson went quickly. Cate didn't find Maths easy, so she was pleased that the lesson picked up roughly where she had left off at her old school.

Afterwards, Cate asked Violet if she knew where the next class was. Violet already had the route marked on her school map and led the way.

The rest of the day went like that. Violet led Cate to all the classrooms and they had lunch together. Violet was particular about many things, Cate learnt. She brushed her teeth after lunch and went to the bathroom to wash her hands a lot.

They bought lunch from the canteen. The food was better than at Cate's old school, with fresh sandwiches and salads, not just heated-up frozen food. Violet smelt her lunch before eating it, then broke the sandwich up into small pieces. She managed to eat the sandwich quicker than Cate, which was surprising as it seemed all she was doing was fiddling with it.

Over lunch, Violet told Cate how she had moved to Dalesea from Manchester when her father took a new job at the local university. Like Cate, Violet was sad to leave her old friends, but happy to be living in Dalesea as her parents had finally agreed to buy her a horse.

Cate couldn't believe it. She'd met someone who rode horses on her first day! Violet had been having riding lessons for three years and begging her parents for her own horse. With her dad's promotion as a professor, and moving to the country her parents had finally given in.

Cate and Violet spent the rest of lunch and any free time talking about possible horse breeds, colours, and sizes that Violet could buy. The awkwardness that Cate had felt earlier mostly disappeared, and they bonded over their shared passion of horses.

The rest of their classes were mostly interesting, and the teachers seemed friendly. Drama was a standout for Cate. It turned out that Mrs. Magill from reception was also the Drama Teacher.

Cate was sometimes shy and didn't always feel comfortable acting. At her old school, the teacher would 'warm up' the class by asking students to make silly faces and noises to relax the class. That always had the opposite effect on Cate!

In Mrs. Magill's class, she talked through the *Les Miserables* play like it was a story and asked the class what emotions the characters would be feeling. In the next lesson, they would go into small groups to practise parts of the story and the characters' emotions.

At home after school, Cate changed into her jodhpurs and had a snack before going to the stables to ride. She didn't feel like doing arena work today, so she decided to ride around Sweetbriars. Her father had created a mowed pathway that circled the property and Cate wanted to do a few laps around it. She got a carrot from the feed room and walked to Odette's field.

When Odette saw her, she whinnied – her usual response to Cate and the treats she brought. Cate put her head collar on and led her to the stables to get her ready. It was easy to groom her now that she had her short summer coat, and the fields were dry and free of mud to roll in. Or at least Cate thought it would be easy until she went to the tack room and couldn't find any brushes or even a hoof-pick in the tack stable. Thanks, Alex!

Cate looked in the next obvious place – outside Fritz's stable. Sure enough, there was a brush and hoof-pick on the floor. Inside the stable, two more brushes were resting on a wall ledge. Cate sighed, frustrated with Alex – they had been at the farm only a short time and he was already leaving things everywhere.

Alex was supposedly at the library, so Cate sent him a prim message saying, "This is our new stable and home. Please respect other people in it, and put things away!"

Then she got on with grooming Odette, brushing her coat in soothing rhythmic movements. She put the brushes neatly away in the tack room and wrapped purple protective bandages around Odette's legs. She put a matching purple saddle cloth on her back, added a general-purpose saddle, and finally fitted Odette's bridle with purple blingy crystals on the browband.

Cate's phone beeped just as she was about to sit in the saddle. It was a message from Alex saying, "Sorry sis. You are right. I am completely hopeless. I promise I will try and be better."

Cate found herself typing in reply, "Oh stop being so nice all the time! Just remember to put things away." Before she hit send her phone beeped again. Another message from Alex, saying, "Love, your big brother Alex," with a love heart emoji.

Cate realised she was making a big deal out of nothing and suddenly felt silly and laughed... it was difficult to stay angry with Alex.

Cate rode along the path for about ten minutes and was thinking about starting Pony Club in a couple of weeks' time. Pony Club had been so much fun in Hattersfield, so Cate was excited to start at Dalesea Hills. It was nice that they'd be able to ride through the forest to get there instead of taking the lorry, but Cate wouldn't know anyone, and the new Club had double the number of members of her last Pony Club. Cate also wanted to be placed in a higher riding level group – she hoped she would do well in her Pony Club assessment!

Cate sighed and as they reached a soft grass path, urged Odette to trot. She shortened her reins and squeezed her legs. Odette was feeling fresh and rushed ahead excitedly, but after a few minutes she settled into a rhythm. Cate could see rabbits scurrying along the path, and everything felt new in the spring sunshine. In the valley beyond the Sweetbriars fields there was a sea of yellow flowers, and a strong floral smell, mixed with cut grass washed over Cate.

After riding and being in nature, Cate was cheerful and enjoyed supper with her family. Better still, when she looked at Instagram, she noticed that Violet was now following her. She followed her back and looked at Violet's profile. There were many pictures of her with her favourite riding school horse, Ziggy.

A picture of Beth had been added too. Beth and a friend wore big smiles on their faces as they posed by the school gate.

Cate felt a sharp pang of sadness, but then took a deep breath. She knew what would cheer her up. She would open the special box she treasured and had left to last.

The silver case was at the bottom of a brown moving box. Cate carefully lifted it out and undid the small metal latch to see a familiar mixture of brightly-coloured glossy rosettes which she'd won at horse riding shows. She delicately organised them, caressing her favourite with her fingers and placed it on top of the others. It was a deep red colour laced with silver ribbon and said, 'Champion Junior Rider' from the Hattersfield County Show.

Chapter 5

Cate had been attending her school for almost a month but hadn't gotten to know many other students besides Violet. The other girls were polite, but kept to their own groups, making Cate feel rubbish at making friends. She missed having other friends to talk to and didn't know how to connect with the other girls without coming across as strange.

Cate missed her old school sorely. She hadn't had to make new friends before. Her old friends had been around forever and hanging out with them was fun and easy.

Violet didn't seem to care. Cate felt grateful that she'd met Violet, but she also thought that maybe Violet intimidated the other girls. In class, she said what she thought, and however the other students felt about it, the teachers liked that she took a bold angle in discussions and they encouraged her.

Cate was a little in awe of Violet with her brazen thoughts and views. It made Cate realise she often told the teachers what they wanted to hear and avoided possible criticism from other students. Violet didn't seem to give a hoot about this.

Cate found Violet's habits both peculiar and strangely comforting. Particularly with food.

One day at lunch time Cate got the nerve to ask Violet about it as she was sniffing at her bowl of pasta.

"Is something wrong?" Cate asked.

"You can never be too careful with food," Violet confessed as she wrinkled her nose.

Cate tilted her head and kept a blank face, waiting for more of an explanation.

"I had a severe case of food poisoning at my old school... tandoori chicken," Violet revealed dramatically.

"Ooh not nice," said Cate gently.

"Yes, it was nasty. The food at this school is gourmet compared to my old school!"

"Sooo totally agree. My old school served frozen food most the time," sympathised Cate.

"After I was sick, I prepared my lunch and took it to school each day. Since it was a few years ago the memory is finally starting to fade," said Violet with a laugh, as she stabbed at a piece of pasta.

Cate was surprised to discover this happened years before and Violet remembered it like it was yesterday.

Cate had noticed Violet relaxing a tad as each day passed. She didn't poke food incessantly with her fork any more or pull it apart. Neither did she wash her hands all the time. Cate was relieved for this as she was tired of waiting outside the bathroom all the time!

As each day went by the prospect of making friends with the other girls felt more remote. At lunch times or in the school breaks, Cate and Violet found themselves sitting apart from the other girls.

One day they joined a table of girls and Cate and Violet greeted them warmly.

The girls said hello, finished their conversation, and got up to leave a few minutes after.

"Ruuude," said Violet in a dramatic voice, after they'd left the table.

Cate was quiet for a few seconds trying to work out what happened.

"I'm not sure Violet. They'd finished their lunches, maybe they have somewhere to go?"

Violet smiled brightly and said, "Sure... you're right," and she changed the subject.

That same day after lunch, Violet, surprisingly, didn't know where the hockey field was, and a girl they'd met on their first day called Tabby, showed them the way.

Tabby seemed popular and was often seen flitting from group to group. She had pale blonde hair and was petite but kind of sporty-looking. She had a spattering of freckles on her nose, vivid green eyes, and fair eyebrows.

Tabby also responded to something Violet said in art, and a lively discussion followed.

Alex had been busy with new school projects and made a new friend named Toby. When he visited Sweetbriars one weekend he purred up the driveway on a shiny white motorbike. He made an impression as he dismounted from his motorbike wearing a tight grey T-shirt and equally tight, faded, ripped jeans with short scuffed boots.

Toby had bouncy blonde hair, a deep golden tan, and blue eyes that reminded Cate of the sky on a clear day.

When he arrived, Cate was grooming Odette and he waved to her in a familiar way before walking over to join her in the stall.

"You must be Cate. Delighted to meet you," said Toby, excitedly.

"Hello," said Cate somewhat shyly.

"This horse is magnificent," declared Toby as he inspected Odette, then grinned broadly at Cate.

Cate thanked Toby but was taken aback by his enthusiasm and familiar manner.

"So how is life treating you in the countryside?" asked Toby, as he stared intently into both Cate and Odette's eyes. For a second Cate wasn't sure if he was talking to her or Odette!

"It's very nice and so beautiful here," Cate said sweetly.

"Excellent to hear. It must help having a big brother as fun as Alex around."

"Um yes... of course," replied Cate somewhat hesitantly as she thought about how Alex was often busy lately.

At that moment Alex called out for them to come to the house as Mum had been baking biscuits. Cate walked with Toby into the house, following the delicious smell.

Boy did Toby seem to like the biscuits! He wolfed down four of them and gave the impression that Mum was the next Nigella Lawson. He complimented her and asked questions about her baking and was surprised to hear that she hadn't really cooked that much until recently when she'd been inspired by her new AGA oven.

Toby gave the impression that he heard your every word, and cared about it, too. They all liked Toby. The only thing Cate didn't like was the way he ruffled her hair when he said goodbye and went off go-karting with Alex.

Later that afternoon, Cate was having a riding lesson with her mum. Since they'd moved, she had been teaching her as Bridget wasn't around. Mum specialized in teaching showjumping and her teaching style differed.

Now Cate was sitting on Odette in the dressage arena waiting for the lesson to start. Mum checked the girth before rubbing Odette's nose affectionately and fixing her gaze on the side of Odette's face. Then she ran her fingers along the cheek piece of the bridle revealing oily grime on her fingertips. "Darling, this bridle is not clean."

Cate was surprised she'd forgotten to clean it after her last ride. She really hadn't been herself lately. She thought quickly.

"Well I couldn't find the saddle soap," said Cate, thinking this was believable as Alex left things in wayward places.

"Oh, is that right?" replied her Mum raising her eyebrow.

She looked at the ground as she circled her toe in the sand before looking back at Cate.

"Cate, you and I both know that Alex is hopeless and cleans his bridle once a month at best – usually when I remind him and am standing next to him making sure he does it."

Cate felt indignant.

"Well why do I need to clean my bridle all the time if Alex doesn't?"

"Darling, because you are my angel who does things right, and I take so much pride in that. Also, don't you think Odette deserves clean tack?"

Cate couldn't argue with that! She thought it was still somewhat unfair, but it made her happy that her mum was proud of her. And it really was important that Odette had only the best, including clean tack.

"Right, are we going to get on with this lesson? I love teaching my little girl again!" said Mum.

Cate found the exercises helped Odette to have more energy, particularly when she went into a two point position, standing in the stirrups and taking the weight out of the saddle to warm up and let Odette stretch.

After the lesson, Cate decided to ride around Sweetbriars to let Odette cool down, leaving the farm along the lane and coming back in at the back of the fields. Cate let Odette stretch her golden neck out into a relaxed walk. Her coat reminded Cate of honeycomb, the colour made even richer by spending the warm summer days grazing in the fields.

Cate was passing the neighbour's house. With the car gone, it looked like no one was there, but as she passed directly in front of the house she could see a window blind open a crack. Suddenly the blind snapped abruptly closed, startling both Cate and Odette.

Cate focused on the path ahead, careful to avoid giving the impression she was snooping. Odette's hooves made a soft rhythmic clip-clop on the dirt road and Cate could hear the birds singing. She took a deep breath and felt herself starting to relax. When they arrived behind Sweetbriars they turned right and followed the grass path that circled the property. On the left was the forest.

After a few minutes, Cate could see the gate that led into the back of Sweetbriars. As she got closer she became curious – beside the gate sat a cardboard box with a stone on top. When she reached it, she dismounted Odette and looked around. There was nobody there.

Then Cate heard a pitiful whimper coming from the box. Odette was sniffing at it, and Cate pushed her away as the horse was becoming more curious and she often didn't know her strength.

Cate took the stone off and tentatively opened one of the top flaps of the box. As she did so, she saw grey hair and a pair of soft grey eyes peering up at her. It was a kitten! Someone had left a small grey kitten at Sweetbriars!

Amazed, Cate scooped the kitten up into her arms. The creature snuggled into her chest and stopped whimpering. It felt small and skinny but had a shiny coat and clear eyes. How long had it been in the box? For a moment Cate was shocked that someone could leave a defenceless animal on its own.

Odette was trying to sniff the kitten, and Cate let her look but shielded the delicate creature with her arm. Cate decided to walk back to the stables leading Odette with her right hand and protecting the kitten with her left arm.

Cate marveled at the fact that she had been nagging her parents about getting a cat only for a perfect kitten to be left at their gate. The big brown mouse had not been seen again, (much to everyone's surprise), and Cate's parents had been so busy fixing the farm and trying to find riding school ponies that finding a kitten wasn't a top priority.

When Cate arrived at the stables, she put on Odette's head collar and tied her outside her stable with her free arm. It wasn't that easy as it was dinner time for the horses; she was moving around impatiently, stamping her feet. Once Cate succeeded in tying her up, she went to the feed room where her Mum and Dad were preparing the evening horse food.

"Mum, Dad, look what I found!" cried Cate excitedly as she entered the feed room with the kitten snuggled into the corner of her arm.

Her father stopped what he was doing and came to look. Cate unbent her arm to show her dad the kitten.

As she did this, Mickey jumped on Cate's legs and began scratching his paws against her jodhpurs. He whined, also eager to have a look.

"Well, isn't that a cute little thing? Whose kitten is this?" asked her Dad, looking miffed. Then he shushed Mickey and picked him up to quieten him.

"No one's, I think. He was left at the back of our farm in a box – someone left him there," Cate said, her eyes wide with excitement.

"Oooh, how lovely. Please let me hold him," said her Mum, joining them and stretching her arms out. She held the kitten in the air, having a good look. The kitten stared at her and began to purr loudly. She looked under the kitten's tail, and said, "Yep, it's a boy!"

"He likes you, Mum," said Cate laughing.

"I guess he does – how adorable. Are you sure you didn't get this kitten from somewhere else, Cate?" her Mum said, fixing her gaze on her daughter.

"Of course not, Mum. The box is still sitting at the back gate. You can go see for yourself. I suppose it's fate!"

The conversation died away and Cate realised how much she wanted to keep the kitten. She swallowed and said with a small voice, "I guess we can keep him, as we *really* need a cat?" She looked at her parents in anticipation and played with her bracelet.

Her Mum brought the kitten to her chest and somehow the purring became louder as he snuggled into her. She clucked and looked at Dad, then said, "I don't see why not, Cate – but we need to take him to the vet and make sure he's healthy. Until then he can sleep in the laundry room. He needs a good feed and a nice warm bed."

Her Dad admired the sweet kitten with his smart grey coat and his loud purr that sounded like Toby's motorbike. He gave the kitten a pat, nodded and said, "Great. Problem solved... kitten found and no more mice."

Cate decided to name the kitten Piper, after the Pied Piper who removed the rats from the German town of Hamelin. (Also the children, but Cate chose to ignore that fact as she liked the name). After a couple of days, she decided Piper was a bit long, and shortened it to Pip.

Pip seemed to like his new name, and within a few days he started coming when she called to him. The family took Pip to the vet, and apart from being underweight, he was declared healthy. The vet gave him a worming dose and vaccinations.

And that is how Pip became the Sweetbriars cat!

Mum and Dad said that Pip should sleep in the laundry room and made a bed for him there, but Pip followed any human who went into the house and was soon spending as much time inside as in the stables. He was a talker and would babble *meow* to anyone willing to listen, particularly Cate. Mickey also got used to Pip. You wouldn't say they were exactly friends yet, but they were often near each other without creating too much fuss.

Although he was friendly to everyone, Cate liked to think Pip was really *her* cat. He would often wait at Odette's stable when Cate was riding, and when Pip heard them coming back, he would jump up on the stable door meowing loudly, trying to get Cate's attention and a pat.

Chapter 6

Cate changed the browband on her bridle to one she'd made, with navy and yellow ribbons which were the new Pony Club colours.

The new Pony Club uniform included a navy polo t-shirt and jumper, cream jodhpurs, and a navy saddle cloth with the initials D. H. for Dalesea Hills Pony Club.

Cate loved that everything matched.

As they rode through the forest to reach the new Pony Club, Cate thought about the day ahead and her stomach churned with nerves. She hoped the people would be friendlier than the girls at her school and her riding assessment would go well.

Not before long, they arrived at the grounds. They could see lorries and horse trailers piling into the carpark and people leading horses around getting ready.

Mum and Dad were waiting for them at the gate with Mickey on a leash – a rare occurrence. Mickey was quite the explorer and at the stables he was usually free, running in and out of the hedges looking for rabbits.

Their parents explained that they needed to go to the club house for the Pony Club commencement speech.

Horses of every shape, size, and colour huddled together outside the club house, waiting with their riders. There was a friendly atmosphere.

Cate and Alex stood Odette and Fritz in the second row at the end of a line of horses. Once they were there, a lady from the Pony Club introduced herself.

"Welcome riders and a very special welcome to our new members! For those of you that don't know me, I am Mands Barton," she trilled.

She looked about the same age as Cate's parents, with short blonde hair that curled into ringlets around her scalp and wore conservative, silver-rimmed glasses.

Mands explained the different riding groups and the order of the day, which was similar to Cate's last Pony Club.

As she talked she gestured with her hands and moved around a lot. Her curls bounced along with her movement and Cate found herself captivated.

Mands' face was void of emotion suddenly, and she changed to a more serious tone.

"It is of the utmost importance that you listen to the instructors and be punctual as there are over sixty members in the Pony Club," she cautioned.

All the riders were silent as her words washed over them.

Mands' face then broke into a larger than life smile as she said, "Now new members, I welcome

you to come to the front as I would like to introduce you to our club."

Standing at the front of the group Mands called
out each rider and horse's name. When it was
Cate's turn, she smiled and waved at the large
group shyly. She was relieved when the introductions were over.

To start the day, the new members were to
have their riding assessment, and afterwards they
would go into their allocated riding level groups.
Mands directed them to the dressage arena at the
bottom of the Pony Club grounds and said an instructor named Benji would meet them there.

The new members walked as a group to the
arena that Mands pointed out, and Cate noticed
that Odette and Fritz were the biggest horses in
the group, (although technically Odette was still
scraping in as a pony at fourteen hands high). The
two other riders were young children riding teeny
ponies.

When they arrived at the arena, there was a
man waiting for them, sitting on a bench. He was
tall and wore bright blue trainers, jeans, a grey T-
shirt, and a blue and orange checked scarf was
knotted around his neck. He had greying hair that
framed a boyish face with grey eyes.

"Welcome, riders – you must be our new members," Benji said gallantly.

The group nodded their heads. Only Cate and
Alex said "Yes" aloud. The younger riders looked
timid.

"I'm Benji, and I'll be assessing you and your horses to put you in the most appropriate riding group. I'd like to see the older riders and horses first, and then the younger riders can go together. But first, please tell me your names, your horses' names, and what you do with your horses."

The responses were mixed; the two younger riders mainly attended Pony Club and rode at home. Alex and Cate had explained how they did a variety of things including competitions.

"Who would like to go first?" said Benji, when it was time for the riding assessment. He looked at Alex and Cate.

"I can go first," volunteered Alex.

"OK. What level of show-jumping do you do with this horse? What are your ambitions?" asked Benji in a serious tone, looking Alex and Fritz up and down, then checking the girth to make sure it was tight.

"We're jumping Novice. I'd like to jump and compete in Discovery classes this year."

Benji asked Alex to walk, trot, and canter around the arena. Then he asked Alex to jump over a cross rail. When he could see that they were competent at the basics, he raised the jump to about one metre. Alex and Fritz jumped cleanly and effortlessly.

"OK, thank you, Alex – that's enough, I don't want to tire you out. You and Fritz are a lovely pair to watch. For rally days and training, you will ride in the A group – the top jumping group."

Alex beamed and patted Fritz's neck affectionately. This was going up a level for Alex, and he was looking forward to the challenge of a higher group.

Benji looked at his clipboard with the list of riders' names, then at Cate. He patted Odette's neck and said, "Catelyn it's your turn now. What are your plans with this gorgeous horse?"

"It's Cate – everyone calls me Cate," Cate said politely and took a deep breath in anticipation.

"OK, Cate it is," said Benji dryly, as he put his hands behind his head with a blank expression.

Cate answered carefully, "Well I like competing in horse shows entering best rider classes and Show Hunter classes for Odette. Last year I won the Champion Rider title for my age group for our County. I guess I'd like to win the Champion rider title again in this county and at the Pony Club Championships."

Benji smiled with his mouth, but his eyes stayed serious. "Wonderful. That's a great goal to aim for," he said in an even tone. He then leant over and tightened a strap of Odette's brushing boot, before adding, "Let's see you work." He clapped his hands together and pursed his lips, looking towards the arena.

Cate walked Odette around the arena and felt self-conscious and stiff in the saddle. She had to remind herself to relax.

She whispered to Odette, "Please be good," and stroked her neck. She asked Odette for a balanced walk and then put her through her paces, including walk to canter transitions and extended trot. Benji asked Cate to ride over a small jump combination with cross rails. Cate finished by asking Odette for a nice square halt where the front and back legs were together side-by-side.

"Nice. She's a lovely mare and good job riding," Benji said, and then turned to the younger riders. "Children, you should see Alex and Cate as an example of where you can take your riding in the future."

Cate was over the moon, but still waiting for her riding group assessment.

Benji paused and seemed to collect his thoughts. "So, I'll put you in the B group with a focus on dressage."

"But Benji, I don't do dressage..." said Cate, trying to keep her tone polite.

"We don't have groups for pure showing, I'm afraid – but you'll find that the dressage training will help your flatwork for showing immensely." Benji took a sip from his water bottle and looked towards the other children.

"OK," said Cate. She wasn't sure about what he'd said, but she could see the topic was closed. "Thanks," she added, but maybe Benji didn't hear her as he was concentrating on the young children walking around the arena.

Cate was pleased that she'd been moved to a higher group at least... she had been in a lower group at her last Pony Club.

Cate and Alex parted ways, and Cate had time to join the dressage-to-music session with her new group. When she arrived, she could see Mands, directing lines of horses through different configurations like figure of eights, small and large circles, and crossing the diagonal. Mands spotted Cate on the edge of the field and waved her over.

Cate joined the session and rode through various configurations with the other riders.

There was a girl called Genevieve riding a stunning, leggy chestnut horse with four white socks. Genevieve had long blonde hair and was the only rider to wear a smart blue blazer even though the weather was warm.

Cate was trotting across the diagonal with Genevieve passing her coming from the other direction. The other girl's horse began to canter when it wasn't supposed to, and almost collided with Odette.

Cate pulled Odette back sharply with the reins and Genevieve's horse kicked out, slicing the air close to Odette's face. For a moment Cate was terrified, then sighed in relief when she realised the kick hadn't made contact.

Odette continued unfazed, and Cate was stunned to hear Genevieve shouting, "Watch out next time!" from across the arena.

Cate was indignant and shouted back, "It wasn't my fault. You were meant to be trotting and cut me off as you were cantering and going too fast."

Suddenly Mands' voice, much sterner now, came between them, "Genevieve where is the red ribbon in Lady's tail?"

Horses that kicked were meant to have a red ribbon tied into their tail so people knew not to get close to them.

Genevieve brought her horse back to a walk, "Oh my, it must have fallen off!" she said breezily.

Mands looked impatient as she replied, "Please get one from the club house right now."

Cate had continued on trotting but kept one eye on Genevieve. Genevieve and a big girl riding a buckskin pony smirked at each other before Genevieve dug her heels into her mare's side and trotted off towards the club house.

Cate felt satisfied that the annoying girl had been told off and was able to focus on the rest of the session.

Mands was a patient instructor. It was a challenge to match over eight very different types of horses with varying gaits. It took some adaptation, including slotting of horses in different positions.

Afterwards, they had a pole-work session where they trotted over a series of poles spaced out by the average length of a horse's stride. Cate enjoyed this, as Odette seemed to be more active and focused as she trotted and cantered over different distances.

At lunch-time Cate met Alex in the resting area. They tied the horses up, untacked them, and gave them hay and water.

Violet arrived to spectate as she was interested in joining the club once she'd found a horse. Cate's parents were there too and congratulated both Cate and Alex on moving up a level.

After lunch, Cate was scheduled for a session with Benji in the dressage arena. She and Violet went back to the arena where the assessments had taken place, but now it was full of young children and ponies doing mounted games. Cate looked around and saw a familiar-looking girl on a chestnut horse walking on the path to the left of the arena.

"Hi," Cate called out. "Do you know where the dressage lesson with Benji is taking place?"

The girl halted her horse and replied, "Sure, it's this way. You can come with me – I'm going to the same lesson."

Cate, Odette, and Violet made their way towards the girl. As they got nearer Cate realised it was Tabby from her school!

"Tabby?" said Cate.

The girl's face broke out into a surprised smile.

"Hi, Cate. Wow, I didn't know you rode... and Violet?" Tabby looked at them more closely.

"Yes," said Cate. "Today's my first day at Pony Club. Violet came to watch as she's looking to join after she finds a horse."

"Wow, that's great. Now, we'd better keep walking and talking or we'll be late, and Benji *does not* like that."

As they started walking, Tabby said to Cate, "What a beautiful horse you have. A palomino, too. What's her name, and how old is she?"

"Thanks. Her name is Odette and she's nine years old. What about your horse?" Cate said, looking at the heavy-set chestnut horse with a perfect white star and flaxen mane, marching along beside her. It seemed to be a cob of some sort.

"She's called Nancy. I borrow her from Avenley Park stables. She's eleven, and she's taught me a lot," said Tabby, patting the mare's neck affectionately. "How's your first day, so far?"

"It's been great. The grounds are huge compared to my old Pony Club."

"Yes, it's great here. When do you think you'll get your new horse?" Tabby asked Violet.

"Who knows?" Violet replied with exasperation as she crossed her arms. "We've looked at more than ten horses now, and the good ones were sold before I even got to see them. The others were nothing like how they'd been described in the ad. One even tried to kick me!"

"Oh, that's a shame," said Tabby sympathetically. "I'd recommend you look at horses for sale at Avenley Park, but the owner doesn't really care that much about the horses. I only stay there because I've been riding Nancy for two years, and I couldn't bear to give her up."

"That is terrible that Nancy is owned by someone like that," replied Cate in a sympathetic voice.

"I didn't see you in the dressage to music session earlier?" Cate asked Tabby brightly, changing the subject.

"I didn't go. My bike's broken and my Mum dropped me at the stables late today," Tabby said darkly.

"Oh, what a pain," chimed in Violet. As she said this they emerged from a wooded section of the cross-country course. Ahead of them was an arena where Benji and the rest of their group were waiting.

"We're here!" cried Tabby and waved at the rest of the riders. "Come on, Cate – let's join the others. Violet, there's a bench you can sit on beside the arena." Tabby gestured to a wooden bench under a large inviting tree. "See you soon!"

Half the dressage arena was overhung by trees from the cross-country course. The riders were standing in the shade facing Benji.

Benji asked them to work first together and was critical and serious at times. As he watched the riders, he pressed his lips together, fiddled with his scarf, and took regular sips from his water bottle.

He had a dinky, fluffy white dog with him that he called Elliot. He sat at Benji's feet reluctantly and play-barked at things that Cate couldn't see, probably shadows or flies. Benji gripped the dog's lead tightly with his free hand.

As the group trotted around, Benji barked orders at them. After this they had one to one instruction whilst the other riders sat under the tree and watched.

In Cate's one to one instruction, Benji asked her to do repetitive transitions from walk to trot, to walk, making sure Odette reacted instantly to the aid and stayed on the bit. When their time was finished, he said that until Odette had more impulsion and a desire to go forward, they wouldn't work on any other exercises. Cate bristled at Benji's tone and dearly missed Bridget, her last riding instructor.

When it was Tabby's time with Benji, she worked on the lateral movements such as leg yielding, (going sideways). It looked like Tabby was under-horsed. She was a graceful rider, not moving in the saddle, keeping her hands very still and appearing to have invisible aids.

Nancy looked sweet and honest, but heavy going, sending small dust clouds into the air every time her hooves hit the arena sand. She didn't have the 'look-at-me factor' that Odette did, but Cate could see why Tabby was in this group – she was *such* a good rider and managed to get Nancy to do many dressage movements while looking very graceful.

Genevieve went next, and Lady swished her tail, full of tension as she trotted. Benji asked them to do leg yielding and shoulder-in exercises in the trot to soften the horse up. Genevieve sat straight in the saddle but was rigid and moved her hands a lot, not giving the horse a consistent contact in the reins. In the leg yielding the horse practically ran to the edge of the arena instead of moving laterally and crossing the legs. In a somewhat exasperated voice, Benji told Genevieve to keep her hands still and relax. Cate couldn't see much improvement by the time Genevieve was finished.

After all the riders had their individual teaching time with Benji, he gestured for the group to circle around him once again.

"Now riders, I wanted to tell you that the Pony Club Championships will take place in December, so you have many months to practise. The date and all the rest of the information will be on the Pony Club website next week."

After the lesson, Cate, Tabby, and Violet left the arena. Cate was subdued as she was used to getting praise for her riding and Benji hadn't been particularly nice to her. But she was also excited about the Pony Club Championships.

The rally day had finished, so they said goodbye to Tabby as she had to return Nancy to Avenley Park on time. Cate needed to find Alex, and Violet said she'd seen him in the show-jumping arena when she'd visited the bathroom.

Cate felt bad about Violet not having a horse, so she dismounted Odette and led her alongside Violet. As they walked to the show-jumping area they discussed the day, and both agreed the Pony Club was fantastic. Violet said she was dying to get a horse, so she could begin at the Pony Club!

Cate went on to tell Violet about her earlier encounter with Genevieve.

"Oh, that girl looks like a piece of work. And she doesn't have half the riding talent that you have!" declared Violet.

"Did you see her horse though? Divine although a bit cranky!"

"Well what horse wouldn't be with that girl riding it and pulling it in the mouth all the time? I would ignore her, Cate, just the way that Tabby and Benji seemed to today."

Cate agreed this was the best approach, and overall was glad she'd met a few nice people.

Violet added, "She probably feels intimidated because another new rider joined the group and turned out to be better than her."

They'd reached the show-jumping arena and could see a group of spectators leaning on the rail watching Alex and Fritz glide around the course – it was big, with large oxers, and even a water jump. People were complimenting Alex and Fritz. They even clapped when he finished the course, and it wasn't a competition!

eventually give up and go back to his favourite pastime – chasing rabbits in the brush hedges.

Sweetbriars was to have an official Opening Day in the summer. Mum had gained a few clients through word of mouth and was getting more enquiries each week. However, she was still trying to find riding school ponies, and she wanted to have them in place before introducing the community to the farm. The family's excitement was building as each day passed. They had advertised in the local papers, and Cate and Alex had put notices up around the village.

In addition to the upcoming Opening Day, Cate was looking forward to the Pony Club Championship in December.

Cate and Tabby were sitting in the tearoom looking at the Pony Club website on an iPad.

Cate was shocked to see there were no showing competitions on the agenda.

"Yes, I'm afraid they cancelled the showing classes after receiving low entries last year," explained Tabby kindly.

"Most members said they preferred to enter dressage competitions at Pony Club. For the serious showing riders like you, they preferred to compete in the county shows," Tabby continued.

"But I have *never* competed in dressage before," moaned Cate.

"Well there is a first time for everything and to be honest, you have the most perfect horse for it!" Tabby said enthusiastically.

Somehow Tabby talked Cate into entering both the Pas De Deux, (a choreographed dressage test to music where they'd compete alongside Tabby and Nancy), and an individual dressage test.

The individual test was novice level, which sounded easy, but after going through the test with Tabby in detail, Cate realised it was much harder than she first thought.

One balmy evening not long after this, Cate was lying on her bedroom floor feeling frustrated. She was tracing the dressage test sequences in the air over and over with her finger – or trying to. She couldn't for the life of her remember them!

Her Mum knocked on the door. Cate replied, "Come in," in a sulky voice.

"What are you doing?" asked Mum.

"What does it look like?" Cate retorted.

Her mum had no idea and looked mystified seeing Cate lying on the ground tracing her finger in the air.

"Your supper is ready," she said calmly. "I called you at least three times."

As Cate sat up, suddenly her frustration turned to despair. Big, fat tears streamed down her face and she sobbed. Mum raced over and joined her on the ground, hugging her shoulders tightly.

When Cate felt calmer and her breathing returned to normal she found her voice. She explained everything... how she was being forced to do dressage at the Pony Club, how she had stupidly entered the dressage test so she could practise with Tabby, and finally how much she still missed their old home and felt she didn't quite belong in Dalesea.

Mum consoled Cate and suggested she check when Beth could visit, as that would cheer her up. She also promised to run through the dressage test with Cate until it was perfect.

Cate felt better after this, like she'd stopped hiding a secret. It had been hard, always plastering a smile on her face to make her family think she was always happy. They had known she wasn't sure about moving initially, but since arriving at Sweetbriars, they'd all bounced around the farm with enthusiasm and Cate felt like it would be thoughtless or ungrateful to display anything but joy. She wanted to be grown up and support her parents.

Still, she found solace in having the horses outside and to Cate's delight, her mum had found a new horse for Violet, which she was now trialing for a month. A grey, nine-year-old Andalusian gelding, that was curiously named Spot. Violet's parents agreed to let him stay at Sweetbriars on livery as their personal farm was not equipped for horses.

Spot was a gentleman, although during his first days at Sweetbriars he bucked like a rodeo horse, scaring the usually confident Violet. Mum agreed to ride Spot first as she suspected he was simply letting off steam.

As soon as she sat on him he was calm, and like most Andalusian horses, he had an expressive trot. Spot had been brought over from Spain by his previous owner, who then had a baby. So Spot sat in the paddock for two years simply being a field ornament and going on the odd hack. As a result, he wasn't very educated, but was very obliging and he knew how to jump.

Another day when neither Violet nor Cate's family were riding, Cate decided to go on a hack in the forest alone.

She left Sweetbriars via the lane, passing the strange neighbour's house. Since their first encounter, none of the Sullivans had seen the three strangers, and Cate realised she had forgotten about them.

As Cate turned out of Sweetbriars she could see the red-haired girl up ahead. It looked like she was going somewhere – she had an ancient-looking green pushbike with a phone attached to the handlebars. The temperature was over twenty degrees, and in contrast to Cate's short-sleeved polo-shirt, the girl wore long sleeves, jeans, trainers, and a hat. She was sitting on the bike but had one foot on the ground while she fiddled with her phone. She looked up, startled, at the sound of Odette's hooves on the road. She regarded Cate and Odette but said nothing.

Cate was curious about her, and glad to have run into her again. She had been taught that it was polite to acknowledge your neighbours, so she called out, "Hello there. I'm Cate. We're your new neighbours. Well, not that new, actually! We moved in a few months ago," Cate said with a polite smile.

The pale girl stood quietly for a few seconds before replying timidly, "Hi, I'm Sophia." Her eyes focused on Odette. "What a beautiful horse," she went on, looking somewhat wistful.

"Thank you. This is Odette."

"Hi, Odette," said Sophia, looking squarely into the horse's soft eyes. "Can I pat her?" she asked, sounding bolder.

"Sure, she loves pats," Cate said encouragingly.

Sophia climbed off her bike and put the bike stand on. She approached Cate and Odette with folded arms and looked the horse in the eye again.

Odette stamped a front leg, getting a little impatient at standing around, and Sophia jumped.

"Don't worry, she won't hurt you. She's just impatient as we're going for a walk in the forest," said Cate.

"Oh, OK," replied Sophia, and she put her hand tentatively on Odette's silky neck. She brushed her hand across Odette's hair, remarking how soft it felt. After a minute or so, her gesture turned into more of a pat.

Sophia had her other hand in her pocket and rustled something. Odette saw this as a sign that she had a treat and pushed her nose into Sophia's hip. Sophia let out a small, shrill scream and jumped back.

Cate started at the unexpected scream, then giggled. "Don't worry, Sophia, she won't hurt you. She's just looking for treats."

Sophia's pale cheeks went red, and she apologised. Cate explained it was best to be still and quiet around horses, so as not to scare them. Sophia apologised again and told Cate she hadn't been around many animals in her life, so she didn't know how to react to them.

Sophia gave Odette another pat – looking more natural this time. Then she said she'd better be going as she had something to do.

At that moment, Cate heard the sound of a blind closing – someone had been watching them from Sophia's house. The girl looked at the window and then back at Cate. She said a hasty goodbye and jumped on her bike. As she did this Cate noticed what looked like a doll's head poking out of the cane basket attached to the front of the bike. The doll had a head full of black matted hair with brightly painted lips.

Sophia sped off towards the forest and Cate was bewildered at their exchange and particularly at the doll.

Afterwards Cate updated Alex about what she saw, and Alex said that Sophia's Dad reminded him of a Russian spy from the movies. They debated various conspiracy theories as they did their stable chores that evening, the ideas becoming ever more grandiose and silly.

As Cate was putting Odette's evening blankets on she had an Aha! moment. She hadn't imagined the shadow at the back of Sweetbriars that first day. It must have been Sophia!

Chapter 8

Since meeting Tabby at the Pony Club, she had invited Cate and Violet to sit with her and her friends at lunch time at school.

Many of the girls had known each other since kindergarten the same way Cate and Beth had. They had familiar stories and gestures and knew each other's likes and dislikes.

The girls mainly talked about themselves in the beginning.

One day an American girl called Ariel was talking about her upcoming weekend away in London.

"I am going to shop until I drop," Ariel squealed happily.

"Cate is from London," Violet said suggestively.

The girls paused and all eyes were on Cate.

"You are so lucky to have lived in London," said Tabby wistfully.

"Um well, it wasn't exactly London," said Cate feeling a tad flustered.

But it didn't seem to matter to the girls that Cate hadn't lived precisely in London.

They seemed to think Cate was an expert on all things London and asked her a million questions.

Luckily Cate had been there often with her aunt and was able to suggest some interesting places to visit.

The real icebreaker came when Tabby told the girls how Cate's family had bought Sweetbriars.

Two of the girls also rode horses. Leah had a horse called Mia but went to a different Pony Club, and Ariel had weekly riding lessons at Avenley Park – where Tabby loaned Nancy. Since the girls learnt that Cate and Violet rode horses, Cate found them more welcoming.

Another day at school, Cate was shocked to find Tabby in tears. The previous Sunday the owner of Avenley Park, Emilia, had told Tabby she couldn't ride Nancy as Nancy was sick. Tabby decided to drop into Avenley Park to visit the poor horse only to find that Nancy was being ridden by someone else in the arena! Tabby was speechless as the agreement was that she had full use of Nancy three days a week, including Sundays. Emilia, the owner of Avenley Park had lied to her.

Cate suggested asking Tabby's Mum to speak to Emilia about this, but Tabby replied that it was useless as her mum didn't understand the situation – or horses – *at all.*

Cate felt bad for Tabby as she had to work at the saddlery part-time to help pay for Nancy, and the person who owned Nancy wasn't being honest.

That evening, Cate spoke to her mum, telling her the whole story.

"Cate, if she's as good a rider as you say, I'm sure she won't have problems finding another horse to ride."

"But Mum, Tabby *loves* Nancy. I'm not sure she wants another horse."

Cate's Mum pursed her lips in thought, "Well, one idea could be that she comes to Sweetbriars and tries one of our horses and she can see how she feels. Perhaps she could ride Bliss a couple of days a week in return for helping us in the stables before or after she rides."

Cate thought this was a brilliant idea, but she wasn't sure how Tabby would react. She was deeply attached to Nancy.

The next day at school, Cate couldn't wait to find out if Tabby was interested in the offer. Bliss was a beautiful young horse, and it was rare for Mum to let anyone ride him.

When Cate told Tabby about the offer, Tabby went quiet. Her eyes widened as if she couldn't believe that someone was offering her a young horse to ride in return for stable work.

"I would love to try Bliss!" Tabby said. She took a deep breath, then she wrapped her arms around Cate in a big hug. "Thank you, thank you, thank you for even considering me!"

"No problem. I'm glad you're interested, and I think you could be good with Bliss – he's a cool dude of a horse! I've known him since he was an itsy bitsy foal," replied Cate, grinning.

Once the excitement settled, Tabby admitted she wasn't sure if she could ride two horses and felt sad about possibly losing Nancy. She felt like she was the only one at the riding school who really cared about her and could ride her well.

Bliss was standing in his field with his perfectly-shaped silk ears pricked forward as he gazed out over the valley. A vision of beauty as his bay mahogany coat glistened in the sunshine. All four of his hooves were placed symmetrically together with his only white leg looking curious, resting in the grass.

It was hard to tell exactly what Bliss was looking at, but something caught his interest and he was focused – he didn't seem to hear the gate open or close when Cate and Tabby entered the field.

Tabby paused for a second, her eyes drinking in the sight of Bliss. Cate looked at Tabby and smiled with an 'I know' look.

"Bliss... Bliss," called Cate.

The gelding turned his shapely head towards them, and cast a curious look. He lowered his head, sniffed the ground, and then walked energetically towards the girls.

Cate gave Bliss a carrot and slipped on his head collar. They led him to the stables and Cate showed Tabby where everything was.

"Is there anything I need to be careful of when I get him ready?" asked Tabby, seeming a bit jittery.

"Well he likes to be groomed, and it's easy to pick up his feet to clean them." Cate demonstrated by placing her hand softly above Bliss's hoof, and the gelding politely flicked his hoof up to be cleaned. "The only thing he doesn't like is when you do the girth up too quickly. We usually put the saddle on as soon as he's brushed and do the girth up little by little. By the time he's ready to be ridden, the girth is tight enough to sit on him. Then we put it up another hole once he's been warmed up under saddle."

Tabby nodded and watched Cate closely as she prepared Bliss.

"He is much taller than Nancy," added Tabby as she put her hand on his wither.

"It's just a matter of getting used to the height," said Cate reassuringly as she combed Bliss's thick black tail.

The gelding pawed the ground with one of his front legs, looking expectantly towards the arena. He knew the routine.

"Right, I think we're ready at last," said Cate, as she gave a final brush stroke to Bliss's shiny coat.

Cate handed the reins to Tabby and she made sure she had a good grip on them, looping the loose end safely into her other hand. Cate led the way to the arena, with Tabby and Bliss walking behind.

"Hi, girls," called out Mum as they approached the arena. She walked towards the arena gate and opened it. "I'm Sarah. It's a pleasure to meet you, Tabby. Cate's told me all about you."

"Nice to meet you too," replied Tabby with a broad smile. "Thank you ever so much for letting me try Bliss today. He's more beautiful than I ever imagined."

"Isn't he wonderful? And a friendly fellow," Cate's Mum said, rubbing Bliss's face with the palm of her hand. "Have you measured your stirrups?"

"Yes, I did. They might need adjusting once I'm in the saddle," said Tabby, as she clicked her helmet strap into place.

Tabby put the mounting block beside Bliss and stepped tentatively onto it. Standing up there, Bliss did look giant like compared to Tabby.

When Tabby mounted Bliss, she said everything felt fine apart from the extra height – she felt *very* far from the ground.

She took a deep breath and asked Bliss forward with her legs. The gelding obliged, and Tabby followed Mum's instructions, walking him around the outside of the arena to warm him up.

Cate was glad there was no one else in the arena to distract her or get Bliss's attention.

After a few minutes Tabby seemed to be relaxing, and Cate was enjoying the feel of the sunshine on her bare arms and face as she leant against the fence watching her friend. Mum called out to

Tabby, asking her to come back, so she could explain a couple of things and tighten the girth.

"OK, Tabby, Bliss is a well-behaved horse, but like most young horses he has a couple of quirks. One is the girth, which you learnt already. The other is stopping at the arena gate – if he feels he can do this, he will, and he'll do it very suddenly. You need to be aware, as I don't want you to go over the handlebars. Usually it happens when he's getting tired of working!" said Mum with a laugh. "Just make sure you keep your leg on him if you feel him backing off. Make him respect you – once he respects you, he's easy peasy."

"OK," replied Tabby positively.

"Why don't you trot and canter Bliss each direction? Ask him to go on the bit – ask with a half-halt and keep a still hand with consistent contact."

Tabby nodded and started walking Bliss, and the gelding started to over-track in the walk and soften his neck onto the bit. Then she asked for trot and a canter. At first Tabby looked like she was unsteady in the saddle, but she seemed to find her balance and look more in tune with Bliss.

Tabby prepared Bliss to canter, sitting deeply for a couple of trot strides and he did a nice transition. They cantered around the arena smoothly.

"Tabby, he looks good, but don't lose the balance in the corners – make sure he goes into them and keeps his balance. Half halt as you approach the corner, and place your weight a little to the outside," said Cate's Mum.

Tabby did as she said and the canter improved. She asked the gelding for five metre loops off the outside track of the arena and a couple of twenty metre circles. When she asked for a trot and canter transition after changing rein, Bliss hollowed his back and went off the bit. Tabby made sure she sat deeper in the saddle, with a better contact in the reins, and put her outside leg behind the girth. This helped produce a lovely smooth transition.

"Nice work! Let him have a break now," called out Mum.

Back at a walk, Tabby said, "Wow, this horse can trot! At first I felt like I was going to be pinged out of the saddle – he has so much movement!"

Cate and her Mum laughed in agreement and Mum adjusted a set of jumps for Tabby – a small cross rail and an oxer. Tabby halted Bliss and put her stirrups up a couple of holes to get ready to jump. She asked Bliss to canter around the arena with a lighter seat. As Tabby was coming around the arena and about to pass the gate to turn right towards the jumps, Bliss put on the brakes, stopping so suddenly that Tabby lost a stirrup and got a mouthful of Bliss's mane.

Tabby regained her composure and stirrup, then firmly asked for canter with her legs. Bliss ignored her, keeping his hooves firmly planted beside the gate. Tabby used her voice, asking him forward, and smacked him with the whip behind her leg.

The gelding sprang to life and cantered. Tabby looked relieved. They went around the arena again, and this time Tabby sat more deeply in the saddle and gave Bliss a small kick and tap with the whip as they approached the gate. Bliss didn't even hesitate, and they cleared both sets of jumps.

Mum adjusted the jumps a little higher, and Tabby and Bliss jumped them effortlessly.

"Well done, Tabby! I think that's enough for today. Why don't you give him a cool down by walking him around the fields?"

"Thanks, and sure," replied Tabby with a big grin on her face. She threw her arms around Bliss's neck and told him what a good boy he was.

Tabby joined Cate, who opened the gate for them. Cate was proud of Tabby – she had ridden Bliss very well and overcame his stopping quirk quickly and efficiently.

The trio walked around the fields, with Cate on foot, showing them the way.

Back at the stables, they hosed the sweat off Bliss and removed the water from his coat with a sweat scraper. Tabby offered to put Bliss back in his field, and when it was time to say goodbye she gave him a kiss on his silky soft nose.

That evening, Mum called Tabby's Mum and offered to let her daughter ride Bliss two days a week. In return, Tabby would have to help with mucking out, cleaning tack, and feeding. Mum said she would try to be around when Tabby was riding to give her tips and guidance. Tabby messaged

Cate straight after the call saying how excited she was!

The next day was a Sunday, and Cate was scrubbing buckets in the stable yard. The place was quiet as everyone was away for the day. Alex had gone off somewhere with Toby, Mum was away in Wales to look at potential riding ponies, and Dad was having lunch with a friend.

Mickey let out a whine and a bark and Cate looked up to see Sophia, the neighbour, walking her old green bike towards her. For once she wasn't covered from head to toe in clothes. Instead she was wearing navy shorts, revealing ghost white legs, and a bright pink vest top that showed off thin arms with a spatter of freckles on her shoulders and forearms.

"Cate! Hi, it's me, Sophia," she said, peering through her thick, black-rimmed glasses.

"Hi," replied Cate, a bit surprised to see her. "Is everything all right?"

"Yes, it certainly is. I hope you don't mind, I brought Odette carrots. I read that horses like carrots," said Sophia. She held out a large bag of carrots from her backpack, like a peace offering.

Cate was surprised, then thought how nice it was.

"Sophia, you are absolutely right. Horses, and especially Odette, *love* carrots. You can leave your bike there against the wall... Odette's field is this way."

As Cate waited for Sophia, she wondered if she'd brought her doll. Cate rested a broom against the wall and looked casually in the basket. Sure enough the doll was there.

This time Cate could see it properly. It was an old-fashioned Asian doll wearing an oriental silk dress. It had eyes that rolled open and shut and black matted hair on its head. It was eerily lifelike.

She wasn't sure how to ask Sophia about it, but she knew she wouldn't be able to resist for long – it was pretty unusual to carry a doll with you at Sophia's age.

At Odette's field, Sophia's eyes lit up as if it was Christmas. Odette greeted them at the gate and seemed to like Sophia and the carrots, which was no surprise, and she let Sophia rub her face and pat her neck.

Sophia leant against the gate once the carrots had been eaten. She pulled out an old-fashioned fan and started to fan herself.

"It's roasting hot today, isn't it? Over twenty-five degrees when I last checked," said Sophia, looking at both Cate and Odette as she spoke. "You poor thing, Odette, having thick hair like that,"

"Actually, Sophia, horses have smart hair! It gets thinner in summer and thicker in winter to keep them warm," replied Cate matter-of-factly.

"That is clever," admitted Sophia. "Although I'd still rather not have all that fur."

Cate had a packet of Polo mints in her pocket and gave one to Odette.

"Do horses need to eat mints to keep their breath fresh?" asked Sophia innocently.

Cate almost laughed out loud, then replied, "No. For a long time people in England have given their horses mints. I'm not sure why, but it's almost like a tradition, and horses love them. Well, *almost* as much as they love carrots," said Cate chuckling.

"Do you need to brush horses' teeth?" Sophia continued.

Cate suppressed another laugh and told Sophia no. Usually when horses ate food such as hay, (often called roughage), it helped their teeth to stay healthy. Although they did need to have their teeth filed regularly as they kept on growing.

Sophia seemed fascinated by the information. Then she gave Odette another rub on the nose and said she had to leave to help her stepdad. He owned the hardware store in the village.

Sophia thanked Cate for letting her see Odette, and they walked back to the main part of the stable where Sophia had left her bike.

Back in the main yard Cate remarked in a gentle voice, "What a pretty doll. Where did you get it from?"

Sophia smiled happily and replied, "Thank you. I've had her since I was a baby. My aunt bought her for me from Thailand." Sophia pressed the doll to her chest and kissed the top of its head. "She gives me good luck."

"Well, then it's wise to carry it with you," Cate said in an agreeable voice and smiled widely.

Sophia said goodbye and collected her bike. She walked it briskly to the gate beside the lane.

Cate watched her leave and realised she'd never met anyone quite like Sophia before.

Later at supper time, Mum got back from looking at the ponies, and the family was enjoying lasagna – their dad's signature dish.

Mum was thrilled as she'd found not just one pony, but two that seemed ideal. Quinn was a handsome fourteen-hand buckskin gelding – his mother was a Quarter Horse, so he was strong, agile, and clever. Saffron was a bright chestnut welsh pony with a squiggly blaze down his face, standing at thirteen hands. He was the opposite of Quinn, being dainty, elegant, and pretty. They were both well-trained, used to children, and had done hacking (or trail riding), and Pony Club.

Mum had agreed with the owner that she would collect them during the week after the vet had looked them over.

Cate was excited to hear about the ponies and to see photos of them. This would mean they'd have a pony for Beth to ride when she visited, and Cate was already envisaging the fun they'd have exploring the forest together!

After supper, Cate felt more tired than usual. When she looked at her phone, there were six messages from Beth asking where she was. *Oh no*, thought Cate. This was the third time the girls had agreed to talk and it hadn't happened... although the last times Beth had cancelled. They *had to* talk tonight!

Cate called Beth, and luckily Beth answered.

"I am sooo sorry Beth to call you back late!" gushed Cate.

Beth was silent and then said, "It doesn't matter," as if she was squeezing out each syllable.

"Mum was away looking at two new ponies and we ate supper late," explained Cate.

When Beth didn't respond Cate continued on, "The two new ponies seem adorable! I can't wait for you to see them."

"Yes, that sounds nice," said Beth formally.

Cate decided to change the subject and asked Beth about school.

"It's fine," replied Beth.

"My school is getting better. Also, Tabby talked me into entering a dressage competition. Can you believe it?" exclaimed Cate.

"Wow, no I can't," replied Beth flatly.

"There are also two other girls at school that ride horses!"

"How cool," said Beth.

"Then today I saw our strange neighbour and she had a doll with her. She is around our age. How weird is that?"

"Yep, weird I guess."

Cate felt worse as the conversation went along. Not only did Cate feel bad that Beth didn't seem interested in what she was saying, but she also felt mean for calling Sophia weird.

Beth had been acting strange for a few weeks now, sometimes not replying to Cate's messages. Even when Cate sent pictures of Mickey – and Beth *loved* Mickey.

Cate was exhausted, and tired of trying to get conversation from Beth, so said she had to go. Beth was due to visit Sweetbriars for the first time the following weekend, and Cate figured everything would be fine face to face.

That night Cate went to bed with her enthusiasm from the weekend squelched. Her best friend didn't sound like her best friend anymore.

Chapter 9

Cate and Odette were halted under the tree watching Tabby ride Nancy at Pony Club. As usual, Benji was praising them, shouting, "excellent," as they effortlessly followed his orders.

Cate had ridden before Tabby. Today Benji had barked orders at them and told her she needed to be less wishy-washy with her aids. He'd even snapped at her, saying "FOR-WARD, Cate! Please use those legs."

Cate had to admit that Odette felt better when she had more impulsion, but she wasn't used to being talked to this way, especially in front of the other riders. It was obvious Benji didn't like her.

Violet had her assessment and was placed in a Pony Club group. She was in a lower-level group that did a mixture of flatwork and jumping. Her reaction to this surprised Cate. She'd realised Violet wasn't as gifted a rider as Tabby, but she'd thought that someone as confident as Violet would want to be in a higher group. But Violet said the lower group suited her just fine and she wanted to have fun and not take it so seriously, especially during her first year at Pony Club. When they met at lunch she gushed about how much fun she'd had in the morning, doing trot poles in one session and cross-country schooling in the next. Spot was a star!

While they ate, they watched Benji riding a horse in the lower arena.

"That's Benji's young horse, Samson," said Tabby. "He brought Samson to Pony Club to school him in a new environment and let him see new things."

Samson was a shiny liver chestnut with a perfect white star on his face. His trot and canter looked flamboyant, which Benji called 'expression,' and he looked balanced for a young horse.

They watched from a distance, mesmerised at what they saw. Benji rode like the equestrian stars Cate admired, and he and Samson were a picture of harmony.

That evening Cate was studying the wall in her bedroom. The photos of Cate with Odette and the posters of her equestrian stars didn't look right. She'd organised and reorganised them at least ten times since moving to Sweetbriars. Now Cate sat on the bed, feeling discouraged, and Pip climbed onto her lap, butting his head against Cate's hand for pats.

"What a nice life you have, just eating, and sleeping," Cate said to Pip, laughing, as she ran her fingers through his soft grey fur. He looked at her with a 'who me?' face, and his eyes began to close as he dozed off. Cate leant her head back against the wall, thinking... *Should the photos go on one wall and the posters on another?* The problem was, they were different sizes and didn't look right with her rosettes squished in the middle. Cate was inclined to agree with her Mum. She should narrow down her favourite photos, put them in frames on top of her drawers, and keep the posters on the wall. Another option was to move her rosettes to the stable tea room where her Mum and Alex's rosettes were, but Cate found it quite motivating to wake up in the morning and see her rosettes before anything else.

Cate realised she was focusing on the photos and posters to avoid thinking about the day she'd had at Pony Club.

She was also disappointed as Beth cancelled her visit that weekend with no real explanation. She said she could come the following weekend, which coincided with the Opening Day.

Cate had to admit it would probably be better for Beth to come during the Opening Day as she would get to see Sweetbriars at its best.

The next day was a Sunday, and Cate had lots of things to do.

Mum had asked her to ride the new ponies, Quinn and Saffron, and Cate needed to do chores like prepare the horses' evening feeds.

In the feed room Cate was organizing the feed buckets when Alex walked in, sat on a bale of hay, and clapped his hands for her attention.

"So sis, are you ready to ride the new ponies today?" he said casually, as he studied Cate's face.

"Sure, they are as cute as pie! It should be fun." Cate said in an upbeat voice as she continued to scoop chaff and pellets into the horses' feed buckets.

"How did you find Pony Club yesterday?" asked Alex nonchalantly.

"It was good," replied Cate, keeping her eyes focused on what she was doing.

"Really?" Alex said, and Cate looked up and met his gaze.

Lately Cate and Alex hadn't talked about anything meaningful. Alex was always busy and seemed to find his new life fun and easy. At least that's what Cate thought.

"Well," Cate said sighing. She sat on another bale of hay opposite Alex and crossed her arms. "It was ok. I'm just finding it a bit hard as Benji doesn't like me very much."

Alex hesitated before responding, "Why exactly do you think he doesn't like you?"

"Because he seems frustrated with me and is always telling me to get Odette more forward before we can do any interesting exercises. Then we run out of time by the time she is going better."

"What exercises does he make you do to get her more forward?"

"Transitions, transitions, transitions! Walk to trot, trot to canter, and canter to trot. He also tells me to vary the trot, going from working trot to medium trot, across the diagonal or down the long side of the arena."

"Hmmm. I can see how that would be repetitive. How does Odette feel afterwards?"

"Better, actually," Cate admitted. "I feel like I don't need to nag her with my leg all the time."

"So it's good then that Benji is making you ride like this... maybe?" Alex asked with a boyish grin.

"I guess I'm just feeling frustrated. Everything feels hard now, and I miss Bridget."

"Cate, do you think maybe you've been used to the same teacher telling you how good you are for quite some time, but you aren't achieving anything new or different?"

Without waiting for an answer, he continued earnestly. "I was riding through the cross-country course yesterday and caught some of your lesson with Benji. Odette looked the best I had ever seen her."

Cate was happily surprised after her brother's compliment and grinned at him.

"OK, thanks, Alex. I guess I'm going to need more time to get used to everything."

"Yep, exactly – that's it," Alex said encouragingly as he stood up and patted Cate's shoulder.

Cate laughed as she watched her brother leave the feed room.

After talking to Alex, Cate felt more optimistic and walked with a sense of purpose to the field to where Quinn and Saffron were grazing. They'd put the ponies together as their former owner said they were used to it.

Cate thought she would start with Quinn, the bigger of the two. When she approached him in the field he seemed to size her up with his clever-looking Quarter Horse eyes following her every step.

Saffron was a few metres off, grazing with one eye on Cate and Quinn. As Cate led Quinn away towards the gate, Saffron let out a high-pitched whinny and cantered frantically after them, catching up to his friend at the gate.

Cate laughed, realising Saffron was worried about being left alone. "It's OK," she soothed.

However, Saffron was right up behind Quinn's tail. Cate couldn't get him to back off so she could lead Quinn out of the field safely. Alex was watching what was happening from the stables and came over to help, holding Saffron back, so Cate and Quinn could leave.

"Poor things," said Cate. "Saffron is worried about his friend leaving."

"I guess these two have been friends for some time," remarked Alex, as he patted Saffron reassuringly and gave him a mint.

Cate lead a reluctant Quinn to the stable. As she looked behind her to the field, Saffron was galloping along the fence line, letting out high-pitched whinnies of despair. Flute and Jambo, Sweetbriars' baby horses, were in the field behind Saffron, and they got worked up, cantering and bucking excitedly along the fence line.

Alex went to the field and gave them hay to calm them down while Cate got Quinn ready to ride. When Quinn was tacked up, Cate tried to lead him to the arena, but instead of turning right he wanted to go left, back to the field. Alex tapped him with a lungeing whip and finally they got the reluctant pony into the arena.

When Alex and Cate told their Mum what had happened, she laughed and said, "I'm sure they'll settle down."

No such luck. Quinn refused to go into any part of the arena that was not on the left, the side closest to Saffron. It was hard work for Cate riding him.

Alex suggested bringing Saffron to the edge of the arena to pacify Quinn, and since it had only been a few days since the ponies arrived, their Mum reluctantly agreed.

This worked like a charm, and Quinn's behaviour became impeccable. He did everything Cate asked and she was impressed with how balanced he was, going effortlessly into canter from walk, and into walk from canter. Cate hadn't ridden a Quarter Horse before.

When Cate rode Saffron, the same thing happened. He didn't want to go into one side of the arena, so Alex brought Quinn to the gate and held him there. After that, Saffron was willing.

Cate couldn't help finding it funny and cute that the ponies were such good friends. But it was also impractical, as it just wasn't possible to keep them together all the time!

Mum suggested separating the ponies little by little and putting the younger Saffron in the field with Maggie. That way, the ponies could see each other without actually being together. The motherly Maggie would keep an eye on Saffron.

Later that day, Cate practised her dressage test with her mum, and it wasn't the best. Mum called out the test directions and the changes in movement came up quickly. Cate was doing the movement late in every part of the test. When halting for the entry to salute the judge, Odette wouldn't stay still and became jumpy. During one attempt Odette even reared up, standing vertically on her back legs and pausing in midair. She reared so high, Cate was frightened she would tip over backwards.

The goal of the test was to be in harmony with the horse, and instead of this, Cate produced a choppy test, that felt just awful, with a non-existent halt at the entry and finish.

Mum attempted to console her afterwards whilst Cate was taking off Odette's tack.

"When Odette reared, she was most likely trying to tell you something," Mum said as she leaned on the fence of the stall. "Horses can be like children. They require loads of patience, love, and training. But mark my words... in time they will give you their trust and respect, and you will always learn something new."

Cate paused in thought and replied carefully, "I guess she is sick of dressage too."

Mum laughed and said, "Maybe. Anyway, Cate don't be so hard on yourself. Give Odette some variety with going in the forest and jumping, and I'm sure she will be brilliant. Most importantly remember to have fun!"

Cate wanted to believe her, but she felt anxious about it still.

During the week, Cate went to the library with Tabby and Violet after school to study. Violet was a Maths ace and helped them through some of the harder practice questions.

They went to the CreamCakes cafe afterwards for iced chocolate and scones. Tabby couldn't resist ordering a red velvet cupcake and somehow managed to eat three scones as well.

They had been to the cafe quite a few times before and knew the owner, George. He was an older man with greying hair that revealed a bald patch when he leant forward to make drinks.

George was chatty. He called them 'The Cream-Cakes Trio' when they arrived, which was cheesy but made them laugh. He mentioned random things like an antique car show taking place somewhere in England and enjoyed debating possible weather scenarios for the day. He was nice and offered the girls an extra scoop of ice cream in their ice chocolate since it was a hot day.

Once they were seated they talked about the usual subject – horses!

"I'm worried about the dressage test. Odette has never reared, so it was pretty scary. She went right up standing vertically on her back legs," Cate revealed.

The girls sympathized, shaking their heads.

"It's probably because you've been practising the dressage test so much, and Odette is getting tired of it," said Tabby knowledgeably.

Cate thought for a few seconds before replying.

"That makes sense. I guess I need to practise the test less," sighed Cate.

Cate suddenly felt guilty that she'd put so much pressure on the mare.

"Don't worry Cate. Dressage is *so* not easy. Have a little break, and you'll be fine. I'm certain of it," said Tabby encouragingly.

"Maybe you do some showing classes again but in this county?" suggested Violet.

Sweetbriars

"I thought about that," admitted Cate. "But with starting at a new school and Pony Club, and helping get Sweetbriars ready, I just haven't had the time. I guess I will go again next year, and until then, focus on dressage," Cate said laughing.

"How is Spot?" Tabby asked Violet.

"Oh he is so much fun! Since I started carrying a crop he isn't lazy at all, and I hardly even use it now. I can't wait to start jumping lessons on him."

"How about Bliss?" asked Violet.

"He is such a sweet horse and so different from Nancy. He is so talented!" gushed Tabby. "The only hard part for me now is not having enough time! Riding two horses, working at the saddlery, and at Sweetbriars is exhausting. Then I am riding my bike all over Dalesea as my Mum is always busy," moaned Tabby.

Cate had thought Tabby's life was perfect as she had so many friends and was such a good rider, but realised how hard it must be to fit all this in, and wondered how she managed it.

Before they left the cafe, Cate casually asked Tabby about Genevieve at the Pony Club.

"Oh I wouldn't spend much time thinking about her," laughed Tabby. "When she began at our Pony Club she used to look down on me as I loaned Nancy and didn't have my own posh horse."

"How outrageous!" cried Violet.

"Yes," sighed Tabby. "But then I realised she has a horse like a Ferrari and can't ride it."

"Her horse is beautiful but grumpy," said Cate.

"Yes, it's such a pity," agreed Tabby. "She also doesn't have many friends besides Gilly, who's like her puppy dog. If you ignore her she leaves you alone, and then after a while she'll probably try and be friends with you. That's what happened with me but I don't want a friend who's mean and arrogant, so I keep her at arm's length."

Chapter 10

The air conditioning was buzzing loudly as Cate sat at her school desk, staring at the large clock above the white board. The class was eleven minutes into their practice Maths exam – meaning they had forty-nine minutes to finish. Cate's hands felt clammy as she flicked through the paper, and her mind was cloudy. The last two questions were tricky. Should she start with them? Cate decided it was better to get the easy questions out of the way. If she got those right, at least she should pass.

As she tackled the easier questions, she began to relax, and her mind went into calculation mode. When there were twenty-nine minutes left, Cate glanced at Violet, and she seemed to be finished. She was scanning her paper with a bored look on her face as she twirled a loose strand of hair around her finger.

"Focus," Cate told herself, panicking slightly. Her hands were sweating again. She had to finish the last two questions, working through parts A to C. She began to work furiously, scribbling calculations on the blank paper, and then writing the finished answers as neatly as possible on the answer sheet.

When she was finished she took a deep breath and wiped her palms on her skirt. Miss Dixon's voice sliced through the air: "Time is up. Please turn your papers face down on the desk and pack up your things."

Cate still didn't really enjoy Maths, but she'd felt it was easier since getting Violet's help at the library. One thing she did like was that it wasn't subjective. You were either right or you were wrong.

Once they were outside the classroom Violet asked Cate how she found the test.

"I don't think I'll get top marks, but thanks to your help, I found it easier than usual, despite my mental block at the beginning." Cate rolled her eyes then smiled.

"No problem! You helped me so much with Spot, I'm glad I can help you back somehow," said Violet, as she hugged Cate's shoulders.

Cate had a spring in her step after the Maths class. The summer holidays were upon them, and the Opening Day was this weekend!

After school, Cate and Alex talked to their Mum about the Opening Day, as they planned to show the Sweetbriars horses in action. They agreed that Alex and their Mum would take their horses around a set of show-jumps. Cate would put Odette through her paces, showing the basic gaits of a horse – walk, trot, and canter. She would also show medium and extended variations where

Odette would cover more ground and have more power.

Beth was due to arrive into the train station early evening and Cate and her mum went to collect her in the car. Cate felt unsure about seeing Beth after their awkward phone call but pushed it from her mind.

As they walked towards the platform, they could see Beth waiting, looking questioningly around the station and at her phone.

"Beth!" called Cate enthusiastically, waving her hand.

"Ahhhh, Cate – there you are!" cried Beth, as she spotted her friend and ran towards her. The girls hugged and laughed.

"It's so nice to see you, Beth," Cate's Mum said, reaching out to embrace her as well.

"And you, Sarah – it's been so long!"

Mum hurried them to the car. "We need to get going, girls, as we have a big weekend with lots to do. It's so nice you could join us for our Opening Day, Beth."

"Yes, I know! I'm so excited about it and finally seeing Sweetbriars."

It was dusk by the time they arrived at Sweetbriars. Cate gave Beth a tour of the farm, and she was amazed. When Mickey saw Beth he went bananas, jumping up and down and doing a dog dance around her legs. Beth picked him up, just as happy to see him, and kissed the black patch on his head. Beth had brought treats for all the horses and they gave her licks and nudges in appreciation. She loved the new ponies and was delighted when Cate said she could ride one the next day.

That evening, the family picked up an old tradition – Friday pizza nights. Toby stayed for supper – he had a knack for knowing when the AGA oven was on! The kids chose the ingredients to go on the pizzas, and they ate them in the garden, enjoying the warm evening that was complemented by a spectacular deep red sun setting over the valley. Everyone laughed when Cate and Beth moulded animals out of leftover pizza dough and play-acted with them. Then it got out of hand when Toby and Alex started throwing the dough at each other, and their dad told them that was enough.

After supper, the girls showered and went to Cate's bedroom. They put a blow-up mattress on the floor beside Cate's bed, like old times, and sat on Cate's bed to chat. Pip and Mickey joined them, with Pip sitting in Cate's lap, and Mickey in Beth's.

Cate wasn't sure if she had imagined the distance she had felt over the phone. Cate still wore her friendship bracelet and was glad to see Beth wearing hers too. Beth led the conversation, updating Cate on life in Hattersfield, and Cate was so glad to hear how her old friends were doing. It seemed like little had changed there since they'd left.

But Cate's whole world had changed. She told Beth about school, Pony Club, Benji, and of course, her new friends Violet and Tabby.

"I can't wait for you to meet them," gushed Cate. "We also have a strange neighbour that I kind of made friends with. I mentioned her on the phone. Her name is Sophia – well, I wouldn't exactly call it a friendship. Mostly she comes to give carrots to Odette and then leaves. She said she'll come to watch my demonstration with Odette on Sunday."

"Wow, you're right – so much has happened to you!" said Beth with a faint smile.

Cate suspected Beth felt a bit left out and decided to tone things down.

"OK, I guess we should get some sleep," Cate said, looking at the time on her phone. It was already past eleven. She threw her arms around Beth and gave her a bear hug. "I am so glad you're here."

"Me too – it's been so long," replied Beth, grinning.

Early the next morning the girls got ready for their hack.

Beth would ride the bigger pony, Quinn, alongside Cate and Odette. Since the ponies had been put in separate fields they seemed to have gotten used to being apart, although neither pony had left Sweetbriars without the other one.

Cate and Odette led the way to the forest with Beth trailing behind, nudging a reluctant Quinn forward.

When they arrived at the entrance of the forest, Quinn spun around, whinnied in the direction of Sweetbriars, and refused to walk forward.

"Give him a kick," Cate said encouragingly.

Beth kicked him, but instead of walking forwards, Quinn shuffled backwards towards the dirt road.

Cate gave Beth her whip, wishing Beth had taken a whip along when Cate suggested it earlier.

Beth gave Quinn a sharp tap on his hindquarters and he looked startled, then caught up to Odette.

They followed a trail Cate hadn't ridden on before that had a pretty stream running alongside it. The day was getting warmer and the trees provided dappled shade.

Beth had been quiet all morning and seemed focused on keeping Quinn going. Cate tried to keep her friend entertained by telling her stories about the forest and things she had learned since moving to Dalesea.

After about a mile, Cate was puzzled at Beth's behaviour. It had been a few months since Cate had seen her, and, apart from the catch-up the night before, Beth didn't have much to say.

Cate's thoughts were interrupted when she noticed that the trail ahead was cut off by the stream.

As they got closer it was clear they were going to have to cross it or return the way they came.

Cate presented Odette at the edge, and the mare neatly stepped over the stream.

Beth followed, but Quinn teetered on the edge, ran backwards a few steps and planted his feet into the ground, not wanting to move.

Beth kicked him and tapped him with the whip but nothing happened. After trying for a few minutes more she declared, "It's useless, we'll have to go back the way we came."

Cate was strongly against this as it would teach Quinn that he had won, and he could turn around when he wanted.

Then she had an idea. "Why don't Odette and I walk around the corner, out of sight? Then Quinn will probably decide to follow and cross the stream."

Beth looked doubtful and replied bluntly, "OK."

Cate walked away and watched Beth and Quinn anxiously through the trees.

Beth was saying, "Come on, let's go," as she kicked the stubborn gelding again. The next thing Cate saw was Quinn leap over the stream, from over a foot away from the edge.

Beth hadn't expected this. She was unseated and went flying sideways out of the saddle, landing hard on the ground.

Quinn realised he was free and galloped towards Cate, the stirrup irons flapping in the air, hitting his sides and making him go faster.

Cate thought quickly and hurried to block the trail with Odette.

Quinn stopped, unable to go further, his nostrils flaring and eyes flashing. Cate grabbed the reins dangling around his neck and said reassuringly, "It's OK, Quinn, everything will be OK,"

Worrying about Beth, Cate hurried back towards the stream, leading Quinn from Odette.

"Are you OK?" Cate shouted.

Beth was dusting herself off. "I'm fine. I told you that whip wasn't a good idea though." She frowned angrily.

Cate couldn't believe her ears. Without it they would be stuck behind the stream, and the whip *was not* the reason Beth fell off.

She was beside herself with anger but sat still and quiet with a stony face.

Beth grabbed Quinn's reins with one hand and examined her arm. She had a large scrape on her elbow that was oozing with blood, and had dirt stuck in it.

"You better wash that – it looks nasty," said Cate, in a measured tone.

"OK, I will. You always have so much to say! Anything else I should be doing?" snapped Beth, as she marched to the stream, with a more agreeable Quinn trailing behind.

"Ouch, it stings," she cried as she doused her elbow with water."

"I don't know why you're so angry at me," retorted Cate. "I have been trying my best to make sure you're happy, and you haven't said more than two words to me all morning. Also, it wasn't my fault you fell off." Suddenly her frustration was spilling out.

"Since I left Hattersfield you practically ignore me, and I don't know what I did, apart from being uprooted from the life I loved, to live somewhere completely new where I knew nobody!"

Beth was silent as she dried her elbow with a tissue.

She looked up after a few minutes – and her face was full of remorse. There were tears in her eyes.

"You're right," she conceded in a shaky voice. "I've been an idiot. I was angry you left and seemed to be having a fabulous time here with all your horses and new friends."

Cate took a deep breath and replied, "Yeah, I have been having a tough time. I didn't want to sound like I was complaining so I only wrote to you about good things," Cate said, staring intently into Beth's eyes. "I also told you how much I missed you about a million times," Cate offered with a small smile.

Cate went on confiding in Beth about how much she had missed her last home, how hard she had found school and Pony Club, and how she had to do dressage instead of showing. She admitted she liked her new friends, but it wasn't like being with someone she'd known almost her whole life!

Beth looked astonished as she listened. "I'm so sorry, I've been so stupid," she said, nibbling her fingernails. She added, "You should have told me you were feeling bad."

Cate hopped off Odette and the girls hugged, then started grinning. Beth had only been at Sweetbriars one day and they were already crying!

The rest of the trail was calm and conversation came easier to both girls. Quinn was spritely as they made their way home – he was either worried about Odette leaving him again or suspected they were homeward bound.

Before leaving the forest, Cate suggested taking a selfie. Beth happily agreed, and they huddled together as close as the horses would allow and snapped some pictures. They managed to get a photo with both of them smiling and a beautiful forest backdrop behind.

Closer to home, they passed Sophia's house and they noticed something curious. The washing line was full of red wigs. Some had straight hair, some had spiraling curls, and they were all different lengths. Cate doubted they were Sophia's, as her hair always looked the same!

The girls guessed the wigs might belong to Sophia's mother as she had been wearing a hat the only time Cate had seen her. It was impossible to tell.

Cate was pleased to find that Beth *did* find the whole Sophia situation interesting. She went on to tell Beth about how she thought she'd seen Sophia lingering at the back of the property the first day they visited Sweetbriars, and it was a bit freaky.

Still, both girls agreed it wasn't *that strange* that Sophia would be there. The back part of Sweetbriars was close to Sophia's house, and Sweetbriars would have been quite tempting to explore, especially when empty with the owners being away.

After riding, they spent the whole afternoon setting up for the Opening Day the next day.

Delivery men from the party hire shop dropped off a load of white plastic folding chairs and tables. Next, the caterer brought a mountain of food.

Grandma Bea arrived in the late afternoon and made a yummy potato bake for supper. Cate and Beth watched television afterwards and then went upstairs to get ready for bed.

Beth had a shower and returned from the bathroom sporting a giant purple bruise on her thigh from where she fell. She laughed it off, declaring it looked worse than it felt, and Cate brought her cream to help the bruise fade quickly.

It was a fine morning, with a few cotton-like clouds decorating the sky. Cate and Beth fetched the demonstration horses from the fields and tied them up in the stalls to get them ready to show.

They brushed the dust off Odette's shiny gold coat, and then Cate untangled the knots from her creamy soft mane. The next hour was spent plaiting the mane and rolling the plaits carefully into neat rosettes. To finish, Cate needed to plait the forelock, but all the activity had made Odette a little jumpy, so it was difficult. In the end, Beth held her head still and Cate managed to plait the forelock quickly. To finish, Cate sprayed a gloss on her horse's coat and painted her hooves with oil.

The family sat on the hired furniture beside the dressage arena to eat an early lunch and then went into the house to change.

Cate left the house wearing pristine white jodhpurs, a crisp white shirt, a stock, and shiny long black boots. Beth helped Cate to fix her hair into a neat bun-net that would sit below the back of her helmet.

As they returned to the stables, they could see Violet and Tabby standing next to Odette's stall. They were wearing summer dresses and chatting animatedly.

"Hi Violet. Hi Tabby," Cate called out excitedly.

"Hi Cate! Wowee, look at you... don't you look all fancy!" declared Violet.

"Yes, so gorgeous," cried Tabby.

"Thank you," Cate said, beaming.

"I wanted to introduce you to Beth – my best friend from Hattersfield," said Cate as she put her arm around Beth's waist.

The girls greeted Beth warmly and said how glad they were to finally meet her.

"I was wondering if you guys could hang out for a bit as I have to warm Odette up now?" asked Cate, as she looked at the three girls questioningly.

"It would be our pleasure," said Violet. "Have you met my horse, Spot? I was so lucky – Sarah found him for me, and he is such a cool dude!"

"I think I met him yesterday. He's so cute, and I love his name," said Beth with a giggle.

Cate left her friends to get acquainted as she needed to focus on her riding.

Cate tacked up Odette and stood back to admire her. She looked marvelous with her shiny deep caramel coat, creamy mane, and plaits. The look was topped with white bandages, a white saddle cloth, and her sparkly browband that caught the sunlight.

Cate mounted Odette, and they walked towards the arena. Sweetbriars Farm certainly looked impressive. The house proudly overlooked bright green fields, dotted with horses grazing contentedly. The stables shone in the sunshine, and there was a floral scent, mixed with new paint, lingering in the air.

The drive was full of cars, and new arrivals were starting to park in an empty field close to the house. As Cate turned toward the arena, she did a quick count of at least twenty people milling around. Grandma Bea was in the middle, offering everyone tea and coffee. Cate could also see

George, who was talking to Mrs. Magill, Cate's Drama teacher.

Cate joined Alex who was riding Fritz in the arena, and Odette walked around tentatively, spooking at the new pot plants. Although Cate let Odette look at the plants properly, she made a loud blowing noise and sniffed the ground, making some of the guests laugh. Cate stroked her neck and let her look until she calmed down.

More people arrived, including Ariel from school and Mands and Benji from Pony Club. Benji parked his white Mercedes convertible next to the stables, visible to everyone, including Cate riding in the arena. A man with stylish shoulder-length hair accompanied him, along with his dog Elliot.

At three o'clock, when they were scheduled to start, Mum welcomed the visitors to Sweetbriars and offered them seats.

She explained their plan to turn Sweetbriars into a fully-fledged equestrian centre, and told the crowd they would even build an indoor arena. She introduced Alex and Cate, who were standing behind her in the arena, and explained they would perform a short demonstration to show the Sweetbriars horses in action.

Alex didn't disappoint as he cantered Fritz smoothly around the jumps. Unexpectedly, he had a refusal at the new water tray and Alex re-presented him, giving him a better line to the fence. Fritz jumped it very big, clearing it with a foot spare. The pair finished with a mock jump-off against the clock.

Odette shone for the audience. She seemed to grow an inch taller, and Cate could hear people remarking on her beauty. She was excited by the atmosphere and her movement was more flamboyant than usual. Cate showed off Odette's trot and canter, going from a collected pace, where Odette's head was the highest point of her body and she carried more weight on her hindquarters, to the more extended ground-covering variations of trot and canter. Odette performed effortless walk to canter transitions, and Cate finished with shoulder-in on the long side and leg yielding from the centre line to the outside track.

Beth had left Violet and Tabby, who were spectating, and had become an invaluable helper. She put the jumps up and brought Copper to the arena for Mum to finish the demonstration.

Cate dismounted and exited the arena. She waved to Tabby and Violet who were sitting together.

She led Odette to the edge of the arena and loosened her girth and noseband. She leant against the rails to watch her Mum ride Copper.

Mum warmed Copper up and jumped a series of small fences, and then Beth put the jumps up higher and higher. Copper's jumping was skillful and a joy to watch. She was scopey, with the ability to tuck her front legs to her chest. As her back legs followed, they tucked under and flicked out, away from the poles.

When they'd finished, the guests applauded. Mum thanked them and asked people to follow Dad, who would show them the rest of the horses and the stables.

As Cate led Odette back to her stall to take her tack off, she could see Sophia and her parents standing in the middle of the stable. Cate greeted them, and Sophia asked if she could give a carrot to Odette.

"Be careful with her," said Sophia's stepfather gruffly, as Odette ate politely from Sophia's hand.

"She's fine. I bring her carrots all the time," said Sophia impatiently. "Isn't she just the most beautiful thing you've ever seen? She was incredible today."

"Yes, I guess so," her stepfather conceded stiffly, looking towards the car park. "Sophia, we need to get going to the village to check on the shop."

Sophia's eyes narrowed, and her face went carefully blank. She gave Odette a pat and then they left.

The rest of the day passed in a happy blur for Cate. Benji even gave her a compliment about her riding! He said she was riding with much more feeling now, and Odette had impulsion.

George from the CreamCakes cafe introduced himself. It turned out he was married to Mrs Magill!

Toby was making the most of the barbeque and the cakes and looked as tanned as ever in a simple white T-shirt and denim shorts. Cate giggled when she heard Toby tell Alex, "Nice job, dude."

Dad had to tie Mickey up as he wanted to jump on people's laps when they sat down. He whined for a few minutes, but then settled down to sleep, basking in the sunshine.

Cate wasn't sure if Pip was aware of the day's activities. He was curled in a ball, sleeping, behind the feed room, away from the noise.

Dad spent time chatting to Barry, a neighbour of theirs who sold hay. Apart from "hello," Cate didn't understand what he said, as he mumbled his words.

All-in-all, the Opening Day was a success, and they met so many nice people. Best of all, Cate was reassured that things were fine with Beth. When they said goodbye, they promised to be more open about their feelings and not to let months pass by before seeing each other!

Chapter 11

The days were getting shorter and autumn was on its way. Cate and Alex had explored every inch of the forest and the horses even knew which direction to take when they were travelling the bridle-paths.

The fields were full of sunburnt grass that was green at the bottom but topped with dry, wispy bits. The horses were experts at digging their noses deep into the grass to find and devour the remaining goodness.

With the shorter, cooler days the horses were stabled at night. Now that they had more clients, the family had hired a local named Owen to muck out the stables early in the morning.

Owen worked with Barry on the hay harvest during the day and Barry had recommended him as a good worker. Owen was from Wales and had an accent that Mum called 'charming.' He was cheerful, efficient, and gentle with the horses.

Alex and Cate were responsible for feeding the horses, turning them out into the fields in the morning and bringing them inside at night.

At school, final exams were just around the corner and many students seemed more focused after the summer break.

Cate, Violet, and Tabby continued going to the library some days after school to study. At the CreamCakes cafe afterwards, they drank hot chocolate instead of ice chocolate.

One Pony Club rally day, Cate was waiting for Violet and Alex at the back gate so they could ride to Pony Club together.

Odette was standing patiently, looking over the gate and down the lane. She had her ears pricked and Cate admired them: they were a toffee colour at the edges after the nice long, warm summer. Alex and Violet appeared, and they made their way calmly through the forest to the Pony Club.

The Pony Club sessions were full of preparation for the forthcoming Championships. In the dressage to music session they worked on the Pas De Deux, with Mands making Cate and Tabby a pair. Somehow Odette and the stocky but capable cob Nancy worked well together.

Genevieve and Gilly insisted they be paired together and the leggy chestnut mare and short stocky buckskin pony were also an unusual combination. The mare was in front of the pony most the time, instead of side by side, and Genevieve got cross at Gilly more than once.

There was a session to discuss the fancy dress parade and everyone agreed they would walk and trot in one big group with the first two riders carrying flags in the Pony Club colours. Once they finished two circuits at the walk and trot, they would pair off and do a circuit of the indoor arena at a fast canter, carrying the flags and passing them to the next pair of riders.

Mands suggested practising the pair work and handing over the flags to the next pair of riders. Genevieve and Gilly were the pair in front of Cate and Tabby and Genevieve had to trot Lady earlier so Gilly could catch up.

Cate and Tabby stood waiting for them with their hands stretched out, ready to take the flag-poles.

Genevieve was on Cate's side, and she thrust the pole in the air then dropped it before Cate could take it. Tabby grabbed the flag off Gilly and went cantering off.

Cate had to call Tabby back whilst Mands re-trieved the flag from the ground and gave it to Cate.

Cate saw Genevieve smile when it fell, and Cate simmered with anger, certain she did it on pur-pose.

Once they both had the flags in their hands, Nancy and Odette did almost simultaneous walk to canter transitions and cantered spritely together. Cate's anger faded as she focused on cantering one-handed, the other hand holding the pole. She enjoyed the feeling of Odette's springy steps.

In the afternoon Cate had another trying lesson with Benji. His intensity seemed to be increasing as the Pony Club championships approached. Cate felt Odette was going well, but when she asked for an extended trot across the diagonal Benji shouted, "More! You can ask more!" in an exasperated tone. Then the lesson ended abruptly as they ran out of time again.

Cate felt a lump form in her throat and she held back tears. Fortunately, Tabby was chatting to Benji when they finished, so Cate had the chance to leave the arena by herself. She untacked Odette, gave her hay and water and put a warm blanket on her.

Cate took a few deep breaths and regained her composure, so that she was able to greet Tabby and Violet normally by lunch time.

Much to her surprise, Benji pulled Cate aside before lunch finished.

"Cate, can I have a word with you, please?" he asked.

"OK," said Cate, unsure what to think. Benji hadn't spoken to her outside of lessons before.

Benji led Cate to a seat beside the show-jumping field and gestured for her to sit down.

"I wanted to tell you I'm sorry if you think I'm being hard on you," Benji said, his grey eyes looking intently into Cate's. "It's only because I think you and Odette have immense potential. Both of you are blessed with great talent. Most kids here would give their right arm to have what you have."

Benji stared ahead, then continued, "You have improved, but there are times where you lose focus. You know what the right feeling is now, but sometimes you forget and look like your head is in the clouds."

Cate had mixed feelings. Concern over not making Benji happy, but also hope as Benji didn't dislike her or think she was a bad rider after all.

She found her voice. "OK, Benji. Thanks for letting me know. I *really* want to improve."

Cate had an urge to float an idea and before she realised, the words were out of her mouth. "Benji, would you teach me outside of Pony Club? It's great here, but I only get limited one-on-one time."

Benji leant back in thought and then touched Cate's arm.

"Cate, I would be delighted to teach you individually if your parents agree. I know your mother teaches you sometimes, and I don't want to tread on her toes. Please check with them first."

"Of course," replied Cate, and grinned, pleased she had found the courage to ask him.

On the way home from Pony Club, they were riding through the forest when they heard a loud engine noise up ahead. A few minutes later an enormous green combine harvester-tractor appeared loaded with large round bales of yellow hay. The horses stopped and were startled as the tractor came around a corner to face them.

The driver peered over the large bales of hay and turned off his loud engine. The tractor took up the whole path, making it impossible to get by!

The horses huddled together, shuffling and stamping. The huge machine was making them more, and more nervous.

The driver climbed off the metal monster. As he approached them, Cate recognised him – it was their neighbour Barry.

"Hi, kids. Could you possibly go back the way you came and take another route? I have a mile of reversing before I can turn around," he said, with a touch of exasperation.

"Um, I'm afraid that'll be tricky," said Alex, shaking his head. "The only other route home will put us on the main road, and it's just not safe for horses. Especially at this time of day."

Barry paused, and squinted at the trio in the fading daylight.

"Are you the kids from Sweetbriars?"

"Yes," said Alex and Cate. Violet smiled and gave a little wave.

Barry paused, looking back at his tractor in thought.

"All right, I guess I'm going to have to reverse. It's going to take a wee while," he mumbled. Cate thought the *wee while* sounded like *wee wee*, which made her smile to herself despite the circumstances.

"OK, thank you ever so much!" said Alex apologetically.

"We are dreadfully sorry," added Cate, aghast that the poor man was going to have to reverse the giant machine for almost a mile.

"It's not a problem – it will test my reversing skills," said Barry, chuckling.

As the tractor reversed, the children followed it slowly, trying not to get too close. Spot, who was usually a cool cucumber, was skittish, jig-jogging about and snorting. As it reversed, the tractor made beeping sounds that were even louder than the engine.

After twenty minutes of following the tractor as it reversed at a crab-like pace, the children reached a field where the horses could go into a driveway and finally let the huge machine pass. Barry was good natured about the situation, and Cate marveled at the relaxed attitude of farmers in Dalesea compared to those in Hattersfield.

When they finally made it back to the stable, Cate went to the feed room to fetch Odette's bucket. Pip was sleeping on his favourite blanket on the ledge of the hay loft, and he opened half an eye when Cate came in.

She was in the middle of patting him when she was distracted by urgent scratching noises followed by whining. It was Mickey, and he was up to something.

Cate called his name and he bounded out from behind the large metal feed bin with something in his mouth. He sat at Cate's feet and dropped the grey object. Cate grimaced and bent over to see what he'd found. It looked way too small to be a rabbit.

It was a fat mouse.

Cate hadn't known Mickey to catch mice before. They hadn't seen a mouse in months, but they'd assumed this meant Pip was doing his job. However, this was a little puzzling, as when they saw Pip in the daytime he was usually having a siesta and at night he now slept in the house.

Cate put two and two together – Pip wasn't the mouse catcher – it was Mickey!

Mickey could see Cate wasn't particularly interested in the mouse. He darted back behind the metal bin and scratched madly at an almost undetectable gap in the corner. There must be other mice in there, thought Cate. Perhaps with the colder days they were sheltering in the warmth of the feed room.

That evening, Cate told her family about what she had found.

"That Pip is one smart cookie," said her Mum, laughing. "I think the only thing he's eaten since he's been here is tinned cat food or bits of our supper!"

"Oh, he's a little prince! He needs his beauty sleep, and when he's awake he guards Sweetbriars, as Mickey is always off in the hedges," said Cate fondly, laughing.

Cate and Alex went on to tell their parents about the encounter with Barry and his enormous tractor.

"He seems like a lovely man, that Barry," remarked Mum

"Yes," agreed their Dad. "Most farmers would have done the same thing, but perhaps less graciously."

They all agreed how nice Barry had been, and Dad said he would drop in to his farm during the week to thank him and ask his advice about the mouse problem. If the mice were living in the wall, it might be difficult for Mickey, (or Pip, if he was inclined), to catch all of them.

As supper was coming to an end, Cate asked her parents if it was OK to organize another pizza night on Friday and invite her friends. Mum and Dad agreed, and Alex said he would invite Toby.

Cate bounded upstairs to her bedroom to get ready for bed. But sleep didn't come easily as she was full of anticipation.

She felt excited about the pizza night and having friends to invite over. She was even more excited about the Pony Club Championships. Maybe not the dressage test but the other activities and staying in the lorry with her friends.

When they'd first moved to Sweetbriars she would often wonder what Beth or Bridget would be doing at any given moment, and that always made her feel glum. But now Beth and Cate were back to their old rhythm of sending daily messages and photos which brightened Cate's day.

On top of that, having experiences such as Barry reversing a mile for them earlier in the day, the strange Sophia bringing carrots for Odette, and even George at the cafe giving them extra ice cream... Cate realised that these random and small things made life more fun.

On Monday Cate invited Tabby and Violet to the Friday pizza night, and they happily accepted. Cate also decided to invite Sophia and realised she didn't have her phone number. Cate dropped a note into Sophia's letter box with the invitation and her phone number.

Early the next morning Sophia messaged Cate to accept the invitation. But not long after that, Cate received another message from Sophia saying her stepfather told her she wasn't able to go as he didn't want her out late in the dark.

Mum offered to drive Sophia home – she was already dropping Tabby home, so it would not be an inconvenience. Finally, Sophia's parents agreed, and Cate wondered with amusement whether Sophia would bring her doll along.

That week, the girls saw Mrs. Magill at the CreamCakes cafe for the first time. She said George had gotten a lurgy, so she was filling in for him.

She asked them if they'd like organic fruit smoothies instead of their usual hot chocolate. The girls politely declined, and asked for scones with jam, clotted cream, and a red velvet cupcake for Tabby. Cate wondered how Tabby could eat so many cakes yet stay so thin!

As the girls chatted, Tabby confessed tearfully that she was going to have to give up Nancy as she was exhausted. It was all too much for her. Cate and Violet comforted Tabby and admitted it was probably for the best. Neither of them could imagine working, on top of riding and doing schoolwork.

Friday pizza night came around quickly. To Cate's surprise, Sophia turned up at Sweetbriars on foot as it was turning dark. Cate thought it was strange her stepfather allowed her to arrive in the dark alone yet made such a fuss earlier in the week. Interestingly, she didn't bring along her doll.

Not long after arriving, Sophia presented Cate's Mum with a gift – a red scarf that she had knitted herself. She said it was to thank her for letting her come to pizza night and to visit Odette.

Sophia handed it over somewhat timidly, but Mum seemed charmed and gave Sophia a hug. Sophia stood there stiffly at first, then relaxed and hugged her back with a grin on her face.

Sophia kept her beanie on her head all night, despite the house being cosy and warm. She only ate margarita pizza with a spattering of cheese and declined soft drinks. Instead she asked for plain water and a fresh lemon to squeeze into it. She said the lemon was good for digestion.

Violet and Sophia had completely opposite personalities, and Violet seemed not to notice the quieter girl much.

Sophia went bright red when Toby joked about her wearing her beanie inside. To Cate's surprise, Violet jumped in, saying, "Well, you're wearing your collar popped up. I'm not sure why." They all laughed good-naturedly, even Sophia.

Of course, they talked about their horses, with Sophia nodding along, trying to follow. She became more animated whenever Odette's name was mentioned.

At eight thirty p.m. sharp the house phone rang, and Mum answered it. It was Sophia's stepfather checking to see if she would be home on time.

Mum mentioned the call casually to Sophia, and she looked embarrassed. Tabby joked that her Mum would either not be home, or not notice her coming in by curfew, and how lucky Sophia was to have such an attentive stepfather.

This joke fell a little flat, and left Cate and Violet feeling bad for both Sophia *and* Tabby. Tabby laughed it off, and they sat on the sofa watching music videos for the remaining hour.

Chapter 12

Cate was a tad weary from studying for her Maths exam and practising for the championships, when one evening at supper her mum surprised her with the most wonderful news. She was going to the Olympia Horse Show in London!

Mum and Dad had bought Cate and Alex tickets to the show-jumping and the freestyle dressage. Mum had planned everything and even bought a ticket for Beth to go with them to the dressage. They would stay with their Aunt Sal and Uncle Pete while they were in London.

Ariel from Cate's school visited Sweetbriars with her parents. Her horse, Mia, was going to start livery there in the new year.

Violet had started weekly show-jumping lessons with Mum and had been doing grid training. This was helping Spot adjust his strides and be more reactive to the fences. Spot refused a jump one day, and Violet went over the handlebars, jumping the jump for him!

When Mum ran to help her, Violet began laughing and saying, "Finally, finally!" as she lay on the ground. Then she stood up and brushed the dirt off her legs. "I had to fall sometime, and now I'm a real rider. The only damage is a stain on my new jodh-purs!"

This incident made Cate think Violet was a bit mad, but it also made her love her even more!

The night before the Maths exam, Cate was sitting on her bed studying a practice paper. She felt tension behind her eyes and the numbers were swirling around the page. Pip was sitting beside her and providing a bit of amusement by batting the pen with his paw whenever she tried to write.

Cate sighed and put the Maths papers away. She tucked herself under the covers, patted Pip as he snuggled into her side, and turned off the lamp.

The next morning Cate woke early with a sense of purpose – to get the Maths exam done and dusted!

She got to the classroom with ten minutes to spare and was one of the first students to arrive.

By nine o'clock, when the exam was due to start, the room was almost full of students staring at the white board solemnly. Violet was the last to arrive, looking relaxed and carefree as she took her seat and peeled off her winter layers.

Miss Dixon distributed the question sheet and answer pages. She explained they would have one hour to complete the test and wished them good luck.

Violet mouthed "Good luck," to Cate, then to Tabby who sat behind them. They both smiled in response and focused on the task at hand.

Cate scanned the answer sheet and couldn't believe her luck – she knew how to tackle all the questions. Usually she found there were at least a couple that were tricky and made a mess of them. She took a deep breath and wrote her name neatly at the top of the sheet. She felt clear headed.

Cate finished the test with ten minutes to spare and found her hand was aching after writing nonstop. She opened and closed it a few times to release the tension and read through her answers. She realised she'd made a mistake in one of the easier questions and furiously rubbed out her original answer, then rewrote the correct answer pressing hard on the page. The lead broke and Cate madly sharpened her pencil, then finished the question just as the bell rang, signaling the end of class.

Violet looked at Cate and mouthed 'OK?,' and Cate mouthed back, "Yes," nodding her head and smiling with a sense of achievement.

The classroom was hushed and quiet as people packed up their things, then as they all left the classroom they exploded in loud chatter. The exam was behind them and the holidays were only hours away!

Later at the CreamCakes cafe, Cate, Violet, and Tabby celebrated their last day of school with hot chocolates and scones.

George added cinnamon to their hot chocolates and gave them handmade marshmallows courtesy of Mrs Magill.

They chatted about Olympia and all the lovely horse and rider combinations Cate was sure to see. Violet and Tabby begged Cate to take lots of photos.

Tabby was going to go to visit her dad, who lived in Cornwall, over the festive break, she didn't seem to want to talk about it much.

Violet was excited to be celebrating Christmas for the first time at their farmlet and had been having a fun time putting up Christmas decorations.

On the day they were to leave for London, Cate took Odette for a hack around Sweetbriars first thing in the morning, despite the bleak weather.

Riding Odette down the road, Cate thought about the things that had happened since Odette had reared and frightened her.

In Cate's last lesson with her Mum, she had spoken about the importance of staying relaxed and reminded her that riding was meant to be fun.

Cate realised how tense she'd been. She found when she relaxed and thought positively about dressage, Odette didn't get anxious, which made it easier for Cate to perform the movements required on time. Cate had also been practising the test less and found that Odette wasn't anticipating what was next.

Cate braced herself against the cold. It had been raining cats and dogs the past few days and now it was freezing.

There were ice patches and numerous puddles on the road, and she had to be careful not to let Odette step in them.

The saddle squeaked annoyingly in the cold, and Cate was distracted by her own reflection in the puddles. Odette felt on edge, spooking at things Cate couldn't see. When they left the road, a rabbit darted across the path, and Odette spun and leapt into the air, unseating Cate. She took a deep breath, realising how close she'd been to a fall. She shortened her reins, sat deeper in the saddle, and urged Odette forward with her legs. The last thing she needed was to fall off and miss going to London!

Odette's walk felt choppy and full of tension as they got closer to home. It wasn't unusual for horses to become spooky when it was winter as they spent more time in their stables because the fields were often muddy or covered in ice.

Back at the stables, Cate's eyes were watering from the wind, and her hands and feet felt numb.

Cate was glad to finish riding, and after putting Odette in her warm stable, she went inside the house to have a hot shower and get ready for the trip.

Whilst she was packing she heard a knock at her bedroom door. Mum poked her head in the door and said, "Darling, I have something for you."

She entered the room and sat on the bed, then pulled an envelope out of her pocket.

Cate's curiosity was piqued. "What is it?"

"Open it, and you'll see," her Mum said in a girly, suspenseful voice.

Cate opened the envelope. There were three hundred pounds in there!

"Oh gosh, Mum, thank you!"

"It's an early Christmas present from your father and me. We thought you could buy some nice things in London and at Olympia."

Cate was thrilled. She had some savings she'd planned to use for expenses in London – both Cate and Alex received a small allowance for performing their chores – but this was wonderful.

"I'll be ready at one o'clock with the car, all right?"

"OK, Mum. Thank you again!" replied Cate as she hugged her mum excitedly.

Before they left, Cate visited Odette to give her a carrot and a cuddle. Odette looked at ease after their daredevil ride, and Cate laughed as she rubbed the mare's nose.

Then she heard Alex calling her and ran to the idling car.

They arrived at the train station with twenty minutes to spare, giving them time to buy hot drinks and a snack for the journey.

"Please take lots of photos, and don't buy too many things at Olympia – remember there are non-horsey shops that sell nice things too!" chided Mum.

On the journey, they travelled through spectacular countryside in various shades of greens and browns, dotted with horses, cows, and sheep. It was a frosty winter scene, and Cate snuggled into her warm mac, sipping her hot chocolate, watching the world go by.

As they approached London, they saw the usual urban scenes full of metal and cement. As they entered the city, the buildings became denser with billboards, offices, and neat rows of identical terraced houses. The only signs of nature were bare, forlorn-looking trees with ghost-like trunks nestled into the pavements beside the busy roads.

When they walked through the ticket gates and out of the station, Alex and Cate found Aunt Sal and Uncle Pete sitting at a table in Costa cafe, sipping from giant cups. They looked radiant and sporty, with glowing skin and lots of hair. Uncle Pete's was an even shade of grey, slightly curly and tucked trendily behind his ears. Aunt Sal was a natural brunette, with hair hanging to her waist. They were wearing similar outfits – brightly coloured North Face outdoor clothing – and looked ready for anything.

"Aunt Sal, Aunt Sal!" called Cate.

"My little darlings, there you are!" replied their aunty, leaping from the table and embracing them both.

Uncle Peter stood up and hugged them warmly, commenting on how much they'd changed. They hadn't seen each other in almost a year as Aunt Sal and Uncle Pete had been travelling in South America.

Sal and Pete didn't have children. Sal was a pottery teacher and also created sculptures. Pete was a retired geologist who spent many months away surfing or skiing, in what seemed to Cate like hugely exotic destinations.

They left the train station in Pete's bright orange combi-van. It seemed to be in hyper-colour, compared to the London greyness around it. As Pete drove, Cate felt suffocated by the low grey sky and the never-ending grey buildings, tarmac roads and traffic lights, although things improved when they arrived in Hampstead. The high street, with its familiar boutique shops and restaurants, was pretty and twee. Colourful Christmas lights illuminated snowmen, reindeers, and, of course, Santa. There were flashing stars hanging from the traffic lights, and in the shop windows there were Christmas trees and tinsel.

Minutes later, they pulled into the driveway of the cottage. It was bright white with a terracotta tiled roof and an inviting yellow door. On the door was a large Christmas wreath with painted pinecones, which Sal and Pete had collected from Hampstead Heath. The cottage was surrounded by a wild garden, with colourful winter flowers, and Aunt Sal proudly pointed the names out. When you visited the cottage, you felt like you were in the countryside while really you were no more than ten kilometres away from the centre of London.

In the evening they went to one of London's oldest pubs, The Holly Bush, for supper. Walking through the door felt like stepping back in time. The ramshackle building had been converted from old stables and was often full of regulars wearing tweed jackets, felt caps, and glasses. Dogs large and small lounged under their owner's feet or by the fire.

Cate sat in a wooden booth and had a lovely time catching up with her aunt and uncle and hearing their stories about hiking and surfing in Patagonia. Uncle Pete showed them videos of glaciers taken while trekking through the Patagonian Andes. They updated their aunt and uncle about their time at Sweetbriars, and it was clear to Pete and Sal how much the children's lives had changed.

The next morning when Cate woke, she looked out the window that faced the garden and the edge of Hampstead Heath, curious about the strange noises she'd heard through the night. The frosty wooded winter scene outside seemed still and serene.

During breakfast with her aunt and uncle, who were health fanatics, Cate asked them about the noises. They said it was owls hunting for food on the heath. Cate yawned and rubbed her eyes, grateful not to have owls living close to Sweetbriars!

After a delicious breakfast of toasted muesli and home-made fruit compote, they went for a walk on Hampstead Heath. It was almost eight hundred acres of unspoilt rolling hills, wooded areas, and natural swimming ponds with views over London.

The four of them ducked into a wooded pathway with a carpet of brown and golden leaves covering the ground. They headed uphill and finally arrived at Kenwood House where they gazed at the beautiful vista of London, and had fun pointing out familiar landmarks.

They ate hot pies in the Kenwood House cafe, then walked back to Hampstead to get a crepe at the famous La Creperie cafe. Cate ordered her favourite – a simple crepe with lemon and sugar. It was delicious and worth the wait they'd had in the queue.

They arrived back at the house around four o'clock and were finally about to depart for the Olympia Horse Show!

Chapter 13

Olympia was full of people clad in Hunter boots and wearing Toggi, Ariat, and many other familiar equestrian branded clothing.

Alex and Cate had wonderful seats in the third row. They marveled at the elaborate show-jumping course in the arena. A colourful Christmas scene played out before them on mammoth jumps, and even the sand shone in the bright lights.

The seats around them were now full of spectators, and the Christmas carols playing over the loudspeaker were interrupted by the commentator. He reminded people about the rules of the competition and talked about the origins of the horses and riders competing that night. The event was being broadcast on TV, and there were countless video cameras and photographers positioned around the arena.

The first rider was from Japan. She cantered a twelve-year-old lean bay gelding calmly around the outside of the course. The commentator explained that this pair had competed at the previous Olympics. Cate had to admit that the horse looked experienced and took the brilliant scene in his stride.

They started the course smoothly although the gelding cleared the jumps by only a whisker. At the first jump of a triple combination, the gelding rapped the top pole with his hind feet and it rattled ominously but stayed in the cups. The horse went on to the second and third parts of the combination, and unfortunately took both rails cleanly off the fences. The rider would not be going to the jump-off.

The competition became hotter as the night went on with the first British show-jumping rider making an appearance after the break. Alex was enthralled, watching his idol.

The British rider who'd won gold at the previous Olympics jumped the course as if they were small cross rails, making it look easy-peasy. The handsome bright chestnut gelding was a pure athlete and completely in sync with his rider. They sailed effortlessly around the course, jumping clear, and the crowd were joyous, clapping and cheering.

Cate enjoyed watching many types of equestrian sports, especially at such a skilled level. For horses to bravely jump enormous fences, based on the will of their rider, was a thrilling spectacle.

During the jump-off, spectators were on the edge of their seats as the horses tackled the giant fences at breakneck speed, turning on a dime to make the next fence against the clock. Collective groans, oohs and aahs, came from the crowd. Cate thought of her mum and hoped one day she would have a chance to ride at Olympia.

Finally, the rider who had won gold at the Olympics took first place. In second place was a young British rider who was competing at Olympia for the first time, and an American came third. There was a lovely ceremony, with the winners receiving silk rugs, flowers, and prize money.

After a good sleep (even the owls couldn't wake Cate), and a healthy breakfast, Aunt Sal surprised Cate with an early Christmas gift: an hour's appointment at a spa in Hampstead village.

Cate was grateful but also nervous. She had never been to a spa before!

As she walked through the entry of the spa, Cate could hear relaxing nature sounds. The building had marble floors and counters and glamorous, well-groomed ladies were flitting about.

One of the staff showed Cate to her seat and gave her a list of treatments to choose from. After a few minutes' deliberation, she chose a safe and much-needed option – a new haircut, which included styling.

The hairdresser gestured for Cate to join her at the basins and she washed Cate's hair. Cate enjoyed the unfamiliar feeling of having her head massaged and smelling the sweet scent of the conditioner.

Then, back in the leather chair, the hairdresser snipped away at freshly-washed hair. In less than five minutes, to Cate's surprise, most of her hair was gone.

The hairdresser spent the next twenty minutes combing the hair in every possible direction, as she cut with precision and an expert eye. Cate found the tugging, combing, and snipping of her hair mesmerising. She enjoyed her wet hair being blow-dried back to life.

And she was amazed with the result! Her previously long hair now came down just past her ears. She ran her fingers through her new bob, and it felt bouncy and as smooth as silk.

As she was admiring the haircut in the mirror her aunt came up behind her.

"Let's have a look at you," said Aunt Sal loudly, and it felt like everyone in the spa turned to look at Cate's new haircut! Aunt Sal placed her hands on Cate's shoulders and examined her hair from the front and behind. "Honey, that looks divine. You look sophisticated and gorgeous."

Cate smiled gratefully, "Thanks, Aunt Sal. I love it so much." She swished her head around, enjoying the new feeling of her hair tickling her ears. "This is much more practical for wearing a helmet, too."

"Oh, Cate, trust you to think of your beloved horses at the spa!" said Sal, laughing.

Afterwards, they returned to the cottage to find Beth waiting for them, along with Alex and Uncle Pete. Cate was thrilled when everyone complimented her new hairstyle.

They left the house earlier than the day before as they planned to visit the shops at Olympia and have a hot chocolate with Bridget, Cate's old riding instructor. But during the tube journey Cate received a message from Bridget saying she couldn't make it. She had a stallion with colic, so the horse was too ill to be left alone.

Cate was despondent as she hadn't seen Bridget in such a long time. She wondered with resentment why Bridget's husband couldn't have watched over the stallion.

Cate looked out the window for some minutes whilst Alex and Beth chatted about the Olympia programme they had spread on their laps. Cate inwardly sighed and told herself she was being unfair to Bridget, and she should focus on the fun night ahead of them.

Inside the main hall of Olympia, Cate was jolted from her reverie as they found themselves hustling through the crowd to get to the shopping area. The shops were brimming with everything you could possibly want for a horse. Alex told the girls he would look around on his own as he didn't fancy watching them debate over which girly horse stuff to buy.

Cate had to admit she didn't see anything she really *needed*, but the money her mum gave her was burning a hole in her pocket. She also wanted to get her Christmas shopping done and dusted!

Finally, she decided to buy a super-soft black leather head collar with sparkly crystals inlaid in the nose piece and the sides of the face. It was to be used especially for shows, and Cate loved it so much she decided to buy the same one for Copper, her mum's horse. She also bought a woolen dog coat with a snowflake design for Mickey, a cat bowl funnily shaped like a mouse for Pip, a checked wool scarf for her dad, riding gloves for Alex, and a couple of backpacks with different coloured horses printed on them for Violet and Tabby. For Beth, Cate had already printed the photo of them doing the selfie in the forest when Beth visited Dalesea and put it in a nice frame. She planned to give it to Beth later that night.

After shopping, they found their seats. The arena was empty of jumps and looked elegant and inviting with red and white flowers placed around the outside at the dressage markers.

Cate was beside herself with excitement. Clara Dulceto, who had taken the horse world by storm, was going to perform with her one-in-a-million dressage horse La Luna.

The less famous riders began the competition, but the combinations were still beautiful and talented. The riders sat straight and still, with gleaming black tailcoats and invisible aids, making the horses float like ballerinas.

Much like the evening before, the excitement built as the night went on and the scores on the board rose quickly.

Most of the choreographed music was classical or festive, and Cate found she enjoyed the lively, upbeat music more. It was a good match for advanced movements such as piaffe or extended trot. It was incredible to see a horse piaffe perfectly in time to the rhythm of the music.

Watching well-known dressage riders compete on gleaming step-masters gave Cate goosebumps. She and Beth whispered to each other when they saw something they liked and raised their eyes together in sympathy when a rider clearly made a mistake.

When La Luna entered the arena, there was an electric feeling in the air. *What a vision of beauty and grace,* thought Cate.

The horse danced his way around the arena, his grey coat shimmering in the bright lights. His movement followed the music effortlessly with his hooves touching the sand at just the right moment. Cate and Beth were absolutely silent, totally captivated by the performance. Cate even had tears in her eyes.

La Luna swung his legs into a dynamic square halt, and the crowd erupted into rapturous applause. Clara patted the gelding heartily on the neck, sheer happiness radiating from her.

La Luna was used to the adoration and walked around calmly and proudly as the spotlight followed him, and the crowds continued to clap loudly.

Clara and La Luna unsurprisingly won first place. In second place was a German rider followed by a Dutch rider taking third place. During the prize-giving ceremony and lap of honour, the German horse's canter turned into a slightly out-of-control gallop, and he put in a sharp buck. The rider was unfazed, slowing him down with one hand while waving cheerfully to the crowd and exiting the arena. *Now that was a lap of honour,* Cate thought, wondering how he'd managed to stay on!

After the show, Cate and Alex waited while Beth went to the bathroom. Cate was astonished to see Benji standing nearby.

"Hi, Benji!" Cate called out excitedly.

Benji looked up blankly. His face broke into a wide smile of recognition when he made eye contact with Cate.

"Why, Cate, hello," said Benji, in a less conservative tone than usual. "How lovely to see you here. How did you like the dressage?" His eyes twinkled.

"Oh my gosh, I adored it!" said Cate, as Beth rejoined them and smiled curiously at Benji.

At that moment, the man who had accompanied Benji to the Sweetbriars Opening Day joined them.

"Hello," he said brightly, making eye contact with each of them and grinning.

Benji introduced him as Adam.

"I remember you from our Opening Day," Alex said, reaching out to shake his hand.

"Yes, indeed. What a lovely afternoon that was," exclaimed Adam.

"It's a bit late for you all, isn't it?" asked Benji as he looked at his watch.

"Yes, it is. We'd better be on our way; Beth's Mum is due to pick us up," said Alex, as he glanced at his phone.

Benji looked confused, probably thinking they had quite a journey ahead of them to Dalesea when Cate chimed in. "We're staying at our aunt's, in Hampstead."

They said their goodbyes and found Beth's Mum, Margarita, waiting outside in her white jeep. She would drop Cate and Alex home on the way to Hattersfield.

During the drive back, Beth and Cate hastily exchanged Christmas gifts. Beth looked pleased and laughed when she peeled off the wrapping to reveal the photo-frame with the selfie photo. In return, she gave Cate a simple silver necklace with a horse pendant on it. Cate loved it as the chain was short, and the pendant sat at her neck-line, so it would always be visible when she wore it.

After saying goodbye to Beth and her mother, Cate and Alex entered the cottage. Cate stayed up to tell her aunt about their evening.

"Maybe one day that could be you," said Aunt Sal, encouragingly.

"Oh my gosh, I wish," replied Cate, thinking about how far away she was from this level of riding.

"I read an article about Clara; she worked very hard to get to where she is. She wasn't given everything on a plate like many of the top riders," said Aunt Sal.

"That's true – she really is an inspiration," replied Cate.

Cate was tired and said goodnight to her aunt, but then laid in bed thinking about their conversation. Perhaps it wasn't impossible to become a great rider like Clara.

At last she fell into a deep sleep, dreaming about riding high level dressage with Odette, dancing to music.

Chapter 14

It was the evening before they departed for the Pony Club Championships. Cate shifted around the old-fashioned felt seat, feeling a prickling heat on her legs from the crackling fireplace. They were out for supper at their local pub, the King's Head.

During supper, Cate decided to bring up the subject of getting extra lessons with Benji.

"Mum, I feel like Odette has improved since I've been getting dressage lessons from Benji, and I wondered if I could try some lessons from him outside of Pony Club?" asked Cate, nonchalantly.

Mum looked surprised and she placed her drink on the table before rubbing her eyes. Alex and Dad also looked surprised and turned to her to see what she would say. It wasn't a secret that Cate had been lukewarm about Benji's teaching.

Mum's face broke into a smile and she said, "Of course you can try some lessons with Benji. You do realise, though," she continued gently, "that you don't need to know that much dressage for showing classes?"

"Yes, I know, Mum. But since he started teaching me, Odette feels wonderful – it feels like a breakthrough. You saw her at the Opening Day. She was incredible, floating around the arena."

"I can't deny that. Overall, I think Benji has been good for you, Cate... but don't be surprised if you catch the dressage bug," Mum said, laughing.

"Well, Mum, that's what happens when you buy me a horse like Odette!" said Cate earnestly.

It was settled, and Cate was excited! Her curiosity had been building about dressage, and she was about to perform her first dressage test – although she had to admit, she still felt apprehensive about it.

Cate's Mum started the engine of the trusty old green lorry. They were taking five horses to the championships – Odette, Fritz, Spot, Nancy, and Bliss. Mum wanted to take Bliss along for the weekend to give him the experience of leaving Sweetbriars.

The venue was a forty minute drive away, and Alex and the girls would sleep in the lorry overnight while the horses would sleep in temporary stables erected especially for the event.

Emilia, the Avenley Park owner, had agreed to let Tabby ride Nancy in the championship, though Cate suspected she was only doing it because it would be good publicity for Avenley Park.

Avenley Park turned out to be starkly different to Sweetbriars. The fences were in disrepair, and some of the rickety stables had broken doors. The arena was small and surrounded with traffic cones, and the tiny paddocks had electric fencing that sagged between rotting wooden posts.

Fortunately, they didn't have to spend much time there. Nancy hopped on the unfamiliar lorry like a pro, and off they went again. As they got closer to the championship venue, the roads started to fill with trailers and horse lorries, all headed in the same direction.

The grounds were decorated with streamers and balloons, hanging from the fences and poles. There was a large grassy space surrounded by a simple wooden fence, and, to one side, a wooden club house and indoor arena. At the back of the Pony Club, there were outdoor dressage arenas and a large show-jumping arena. There was also a cross-country course that followed the perimeter of the Pony Club, with large wooden fences and smaller jump options beside them.

A man in a bright yellow vest directed them to an area where lorries could park. It was full of large, bare trees, and the ground was covered with brown and gold leaves that had fallen recently.

As they parked they could see a large sleek silver lorry turning into the parking area. There was an elegant man behind the steering wheel. Sitting beside him were Genevieve and Gilly, peering over the dashboard. As they parked their lorry and jumped out, Genevieve waved stiffly at Cate and her friends. They waved back and focused on unloading the horses. Cate had taken Tabby's advice to heart to ignore Genevieve, but she also knew it was important to be polite.

Once the horses were safely in the stables with hay, Mum and Dad returned to Sweetbriars to feed the other horses. Mands and some of the other parents would be camping on the Pony Club grounds in case of any emergencies.

They unpacked and polished their tack and boots until they were clean and shiny, before feeding the horses and heading to the club house for supper. Large tables were allocated for members of each branch and Cate, Alex, Violet, and Tabby joined their friends. The room was bursting with loud chatter and people were full of cheer.

The coordinator of the Pony Club hosting the championships welcomed each table individually. People clapped and cheered.

A hearty British dinner was served, including bangers and mash and fish and chips. For dessert, they had a choice of apple pie or Eton mess. Cate felt nervous, with butterflies in her stomach, and couldn't eat very much.

After supper, the three girls were lying together in the double bed in the lorry. They were huddled over an iPad, watching people perform the dressage tests Cate and Tabby would ride on the Sunday. The girls discussed the horse and rider combinations, what they did – or didn't do well, whilst eating the chocolate orange balls Violet had brought along.

Violet had come to the championships very well-prepared. Her bag seemed to be packed with extreme care and her clothes looked like new, crisp, and perfectly folded. Her washbag had numerous compartments and her toiletries were clearly labelled. Best of all, she had brought all types of chocolate!

Alex was lying on the top bunk with his earphones on, watching a show-jumping championship taking place somewhere in Europe and shushed them a couple of times.

They went to sleep around eleven o'clock, and the next morning at five thirty the alarm sounded on all four of their phones simultaneously. There was no hiding from that!

They had to plait the horses' manes into rosettes, which took some time. They ate breakfast in the lorry, and by eight o'clock, Cate and Tabby were ready. Horses, boots, and tack gleamed as they walked Odette and Nancy to the dressage to music competition area.

For the Pas de Deux competition, Cate and Tabby had chosen a combination of music from Michael Jackson, and it matched their routine well. They managed to synchronise medium trots across the diagonal, trot up the centre line, and leg yield to the outside at the same time and finish with simultaneous balanced, square halts. In the medium trot, Cate made sure to half halt across the diagonal instead of letting Odette rush, and it helped to get greater extension in her front legs and to be in time with Nancy who didn't have such big paces.

When they'd finished, they could see the judges writing their marks down. Parents and friends, including Violet, began to clap and cheer them from the fence-line.

Tabby and Cate beamed and gave each other high fives. They patted their horses and told them how good they were. Then they joined their parents and walked back to the lorry to feed the horses before the afternoon competition.

"What a tremendous group. And you two stole the show – I am so proud of you," said Dad, as he patted Odette's neck.

"You both looked wonderful – it was amazing to watch," added Violet.

"Absolutely marvelous," agreed Mum.

Cate and Tabby were thrilled and thanked them, but the results wouldn't be announced until later in the day.

Once Odette and Nancy were back in their stables, the two girls walked to the jumping area where Violet would be competing.

Violet confidently trotted and cantered Spot around the warm-up arena, over cross-rails, uprights, and small oxers. Despite the area being full of ponies and riders, Spot was focused and relaxed, and Violet was clearly enjoying herself.

When Spot was warmed up, Violet dismounted to walk the course. Tabby held Spot while Cate and Violet assessed the course together. The jumps were not too high and were decorated like a forest scene. As Violet had been taught to do at Pony Club, she counted the steps in between fences to measure the strides Spot would need to take. She wasn't fazed by most of the course, just a little nervous about the water jump.

Violet hopped back on Spot and cantered him over two more fences before her name was called.

She entered the show-jumping ring and started trotting around the jumps, letting Spot look at them. Once the bell rang, they cantered towards the first jump with the red flag on their right. Spot cleared it, then continued to bounce his way around the course. The only jump he hesitated on was the water, as Violet had suspected he would. She dug her heels into Spot's sides and clicked her tongue. The hesitant gelding leaped over the water fence, clearing it easily. Violet had a clear round! This meant she would participate in the jump-off when the other riders finished.

"Well done – that was excellent," Cate told her as she left the arena. They returned to the fence-line and Cate gave Spot a Polo mint.

"That was *so* much fun!" said Violet.

Violet's parents looked as proud as could be, and she leant over to hug them both.

"Congratulations, Violet – what a great round!" said Cate's Mum.

Five riders participated in the jump-off, including Ariel from school. She went before Violet and took two rails down. This didn't rattle Violet though – she hadn't thought she would be doing a show-jumping course only a few months into owning Spot and was over the moon just to have made it so far in so little time.

Violet entered the ring and cantered Spot towards the first fence which was a simple upright. It was followed by another simple fence, a double combination, and then the water, with a couple of tricky turns to make in between. The jump-off was judged by both time and the number of rails knocked down.

Violet cleared all the jumps until she reached the water. Spot seemed to hesitate again, slowing down to a trot and running out to the left. Violet turned him to the right, kicked him, and he jumped the jump crookedly from a trot, taking down the top rail. Violet refocused him, and they cantered over the last two jumps faultlessly to finish.

Spectators clapped her from the edge of the arena as Violet walked Spot and patted him, pleased with the result.

"Well done, Violet! Excellent work to keep him going over that water jump," said Mum.

"Thanks ever so much! Yes, I thought he would go over it no problem that time, but I kicked him a bit too late," said Violet. She shrugged but grinned too.

"Well, he went over it – that's the main thing," said Alex, who had also watched Violet's jump-off.

They watched two more horses go around, one achieving a clear round but the other having two rails. Then the results were called over the loud-speaker – Violet came in third place! She had to go back into the ring for the prize-giving ceremony. She was thrilled – her first ever rosette!

Next, Mum coached Alex and Fritz in the warm-up, guiding them through double fences with a large upright and wide oxer. Alex was competing in the highest show-jumping level for Pony Club, and they were all excited to watch him.

Then Alex and Mum walked the course, debating potential difficulties and how best to approach them.

Toby arrived to spectate his first show-jumping competition. He was in awe at Alex's bravery as he took in the show-jumping course with its big obstacles.

"No way would I hop on something that big, with its own mind, and ask it to jump over those fences. No way," said Toby, shaking his head, his eyes wide.

"Who knows, maybe one day I'll do it," said Violet breezily, as she flicked back her hair, spurred on by her success.

Tabby and Cate laughed, and Tabby said, "Why not? It's great to have hopes and dreams!"

"Exactly, Tabster," replied Violet, laughing. Violet had given Tabby her new nickname at the CreamCakes cafe recently, and they all found it funny.

Alex began the course and Fritz jumped with energy to finish clear and go on to the jump-off.

In the jump-off, the lines were tight. Alex and Fritz jumped the fences more carefully, and the gentle giant slowed down and sped up where needed. They unexpectedly took a rail at the last fence, but finished in the quickest time, securing second place. The rider who took first place was the son of a top British show-jumper, and Alex was delighted to finish second only to him.

Cate and Tabby went to the club house to retrieve their Pas De Deux results. When they reached the wall where the results were written, they could see Genevieve and Gilly scrutinizing the noticeboard. They barely smiled at Cate and Tabby before marching into the club house cafe.

Cate and Tabby searched for their names and were thrilled – they came second! Genevieve and Gilly's names were also on the list... at the bottom as they had come second last. For a moment Cate was surprised they did *so* badly, but she was mostly delighted that she and Tabby had done so well!

They hugged each other and jumped up and down enthusiastically.

"Wow, who would have thought Nancy and Odette could do so well in the Pas de Deux?" cried Cate. "They seemed such an unlikely pair."

"I know," remarked Tabby. "They were terrific!"

At that moment Cate's Mum came up behind them. When she saw the results, she congratulated them both. Then she said she was going to the cafe and afterwards would give Tabby a lesson on Bliss, since most of the competitions were finished for the day.

Cate helped Tabby prepare Bliss, and they met Mum in the empty arena as agreed. Bliss was excited. He passaged his way around and Cate thought Tabby did a good job of sitting still and staying calm. Once Bliss was warmed up, he was focused and obedient as Mum directed the pair through their paces.

Afterwards at the lorry Tabby tied Bliss to a piece of string attached to the door, whilst she retrieved a blanket to put over him.

Suddenly, a loose balloon came blowing towards Bliss. He pulled back, breaking the string, and bolted! The bay gelding galloped wildly up the path towards the club house, his eyes flashing, terrified.

Cate's Mum was coming out of the bathroom and her face went ashen to see Bliss galloping wildly with poor Tabby running hopelessly behind him, calling his name.

A bunch of balloons on his right caught his eye and he slowed down, then leaped to the left, brushing his foreleg on the fence. He came to a stop when the path ended at the club house and people were standing around him, waving their arms at him to stop.

When Tabby reached Bliss, blood was dripping from his leg.

Mands was there and took control, along with Mum who had joined the scene. They inspected Bliss's leg, pulling the exercise boot up to reveal the damage. He had taken the skin off above his fetlock, and a flap of it sagged over the wound.

Mum wrapped the wound with a bandage Mands had given her to stem the flow of blood.

Cate had seen what had happened from Odette's stable and raced to the scene with Bliss's blanket. Tabby looked crestfallen and Cate hugged her shoulder sympathetically before putting the fleece blanket on Bliss. He felt ice cold despite his neck being covered with foamy sweat.

Mands went to find the vet who was at the Championships for the whole weekend. He arrived quickly with his car and removed the bandage to look at the wound. More blood trickled out of it, but not like before, and Julian the vet congratulated Cate's Mum for applying the bandage quickly.

After examining Bliss's fetlock, the vet declared there was no damage to the tendon or joint, and the most important thing was to keep the wound clean so it wouldn't get infected and could heal well. He said it could be challenging as the wound was in an area where there was a lot of movement, and therefore Bliss would need to go on stable-rest for at least one month. He gave Bliss a tetanus shot and a local anaesthetic, then carefully sewed the wound together.

Bliss walked tentatively as Tabby led him back to his stable. Once safely inside, he seemed content and munched through a bucket of feed. Tabby did not leave his side.

Violet joined them in the stable, bringing Ferrero Roche chocolates to try to cheer Tabby up. But it was obvious Tabby needed more than chocolate to make her feel better.

Finally, they managed to convince Tabby to leave Bliss so they could prepare their fancy-dress outfits for the next day. The parade would take place after the final prize-giving ceremony in the indoor arena.

This year's theme was 'From the Sea,' inspired by the nearby Atlantic Ocean. The girls would go as mermaids and their horses would be seahorses. They'd bought wigs with green flowing hair that they'd put over their helmets and sparkly bodices with long sleeves. They needed to glue silver glitter to their jodhpurs and spray the horses' manes and tails green. The look would be completed by silver saddle cloths.

As they sat on the bed in the lorry, gluing glitter to their jodhpurs, Tabby stated flatly, "I don't even want to go."

"Come on, Tabby, it will be fun," coaxed both Cate and Violet.

Cate's Mum entered the lorry, and her voice surprised them as she leant against the bunk beds.

"Bliss is fine and knows how much you care about him," she said gently to Tabby.

Tabby sighed, and tears pooled in her eyes, "I am so dreadfully sorry, Sarah. I should have never tied a young horse to a piece of string," Tabby said full of remorse.

"Don't worry," Mum said kindly. "It could happen to any of us, and how were you to know there would be a loose balloon? It could have been worse if he hadn't been tied by the string. If he hadn't been able to get away, he really would have panicked and maybe caused even more damage to himself."

Mum sat on the edge of the bed, held Tabby's hand, and went on to say, "Accidents like this make us more careful, and I know this is your first time handling a young horse."

Tabby managed a smile, and found her voice, "Thank you for being so understanding."

Over supper, Tabby admitted to Cate and Violet that she was still worried about Bliss despite the vet saying he should be OK. But she was so thankful that Cate's Mum wasn't blaming her.

Cate and Violet reminded Tabby that the vet was an expert and she should believe him.

Chapter 15

The morning was frosty and bleak as Cate and Tabby prepared for the individual dressage competition. Despite the cold weather, the tests would take place outside. Fortunately, it wasn't raining, and the arenas had an all-weather surface which were good to ride on whatever the weather.

Cate was jittery when she first hopped on Odette and whispered, "I know you will be brilliant," before stroking her neck and walking her around the warm-up arena.

Tabby was doing an elementary test, which was one level higher than Cate. Cate was relieved as she didn't want the added pressure of competing against her friend.

Mum helped them warm up for their tests, making sure they practised all the movements required. Cate felt in tune with Odette after warming up and was so absorbed with practising she didn't hear her name called, signaling her to begin her test.

Tabby called out to Cate, "They're calling you." Cate started in surprise, then rode Odette quickly to the allocated arena.

There was a judges' box at A at the end of the arena. Cate walked Odette to the box, trying to ignore her butterflies, and halted and confirmed their names. The judge and writer peered at Cate through the window, and kindly wished them good luck.

Cate trotted Odette away from the box. After a minute she heard the bell ring, signaling her to enter. Cate circled around the arena and turned Odette boldly up the centre line, trying to maintain good impulsion for a square halt. Odette halted squarely and remarkably still while Cate saluted the judges. They waved their hands, indicating that Cate should begin.

Cate pushed the mare back into trot and turned left at A, then proceeded to letter B and did a twenty-metre circle, making sure Odette was in a forward working trot and on the bit. Cate continued to her canter work, then suddenly she heard a bell ring. She kept on going and the bell rang again. She looked towards the judges, confused.

The writer left the judges' box and called out, "You made a mistake."

Cate was mortified, and her mind went blank. She couldn't remember where she was up to in her performance, or where she'd made the mistake!

Then, much to Cate's surprise, Benji appeared from nowhere and approached the judges. Cate could see them talking and nodding their heads. Benji then shouted, "Cate, I'll call the test out for you, OK?"

Cate was beyond relieved, and called back, "Thank you!"

The judges rang the bell again signaling Cate to carry on.

Cate trotted Odette and thought, stuff it, there was no point in being nervous, she was simply going to have fun since she had no chance of winning a place now.

Benji's voice rang out clearly. "Cross the diagonal in trot showing some medium strides. At C, canter right." And so on.

Cate followed his directions, and as she didn't need to remember what was next, she focused on her riding and felt more in control. She managed to perform transitions on each marker, and Odette's free walk across the diagonal was the best. The horse stretched her head down, relaxed and at ease, striding out smoothly.

Before Cate knew it, the test was coming to a finish. She halted almost square at X, saluted the judges and smiled, then left the arena.

Cate's family were waiting for her nearby, along with Violet and Tabby.

"I can't believe I forgot what I was doing! I just blanked!" said Cate, grimacing and holding her head in her hands.

"Darling, it's OK. It was your first ever dressage test and much of it was excellent," her mother said as she patted her on the back.

Benji joined them and said, "Congratulations on your first dressage test, Cate."

"Umm, thanks, but I made a mistake!" cried Cate dramatically, her hopes of winning a place utterly dashed.

"Yes, but it doesn't matter. You lose some marks for a course error, but it's not that damaging to your result. Your walk was superb, so you'll make the marks up. The walk receives double the marks of the rest of the paces."

"Really?" said Cate, astonished. She'd thought her test was ruined, and now she realised the second half of the test had been more relaxed, precisely because she'd thought she had no hope of winning a place!

"Yes, really," replied Benji in his usual no-nonsense way. "Again, well done." And with that he went back to the seat beside the arena to spectate his other students.

Cate was awfully relieved and smiled at everyone.

"See, Cate, nothing to worry about. I'm sure you'll win something," said Violet encouragingly, although Cate didn't care so much about that at this point. She had initially wanted to win a place in the competition, but now she would be happy to not come last! She hated that she had blanked when she was nervous.

Mum hugged Cate and slipped Odette a couple of sugar cubes. Then she suggested they watch Tabby's dressage test.

At the warm-up arena, Tabby called out, "What a lovely test! Lovely transitions and a smashing walk!"

Cate called out thanks and was grateful for the support she had. She wondered where Tabby's mother was. Tabby had said she was coming, but so far there had been no sign of her.

Cate put Odette back in her stable and covered her with a blanket, then rushed back to watch Tabby's test. She missed Tabby's entry but caught the rest of the test. Tabby rode Nancy wonderfully, but it looked like the horse was tired and Tabby didn't get the medium paces she needed in both trot and canter. Nancy also trotted in the counter canter, which would hurt their overall mark.

When the test finished, Tabby gushed to Cate and Violet about what a good girl Nancy was. She didn't seem disappointed by the horse's lack of energy throughout the test. Tabby had just started at elementary level, and said she was happy to be competing at this level where lateral work and collection was required.

Suddenly Tabby seemed to be distracted, looking over Cate's shoulder. Cate turned around and saw an attractive lady approaching them. She was wearing a dark blue velour tracksuit – the kind that costs a lot of money – paired with expensive trainers and a quilted jacket that had an elaborate fur-trimmed hood.

"Mummy, you made it," Tabby said formally, like she was talking to a stranger.

"Of course I made it, darling. I was watching you from the trees over there," Tabby's mother said, pointing to a cluster of trees, to prove this point.

"Sure," replied Tabby, and she pressed her lips together, then smiled.

"You were marvelous, as usual," said her mother, as she patted Tabby's arm, taking care not to get too close to Nancy. Tabby then introduced her mother, who was called Diane, to Cate and Violet.

"Oh, aren't you an adorable lot? I'm thrilled that Tabitha has wonderful friends like you," said Diane in a loud, over-the-top voice.

Cate noticed she looked a lot like Tabby – a blonde bouncy bob, brilliant green eyes and luminescent skin. Diane reminded Cate of a grown-up Barbie doll. She had bronzed her face, had ink-black eyelashes, carefully lined eyes, and manicured nails.

An announcement came over the loudspeaker reminding people that the prize-giving for the dressage would be at four o'clock followed by the fancy dress parade an hour later. They would need to go to the club house around three o'clock to see their results.

The girls took Nancy back to her stable. Diane trailed behind them, careful where she placed her expensively-clad feet.

Back at the stable they fed the horses, brushed them, and put on their blankets. The day was becoming more miserable, and they didn't want the horses to catch a chill. Diane stood around looking like a fish out of water. The questions she asked revealed that her knowledge of Nancy and Tabby's relationship was limited.

Diane looked at her gold watch regularly until she declared she had to leave to attend a pilates class, but she would return later for the parade. She hugged Tabby, who thanked her mother politely for coming.

At three o'clock the girls went to the club house to retrieve their dressage results. Cate couldn't believe it – she'd come in fourth with a score of sixty-six percent! That meant she would attend the prize-giving ceremony as they awarded rosettes up to fifth place.

Tabby came in fifth place, however, with a lower percentage of sixty-two per cent.

"How can that be?" asked Cate, mystified.

"Did you not see the supermodel warmbloods in the warm-up arena? They were competing in my test as well as the higher tests. I just can't compete against that with Nancy. Not to mention that she lacked energy today," said Tabby, sighing.

"Yes, but next year you'll be able to compete against them with Bliss. That'll be more of a fair competition," countered Violet in a knowledgeable voice.

"Oh, I hope so – that would be amazing," replied Tabby wistfully.

Violet produced snack-sized Bounty chocolate bars with a cheeky smile, "Anyone fancy some chocolate to celebrate?"

The girls laughed and remarked how Violet knew the best moments to produce chocolate. They gobbled it down and raced to the stables to get ready for the prize-giving ceremony.

There were two prize-giving ceremonies for Cate and Tabby to attend – the Pas De Deux and the individual dressage. During the ceremony the judges congratulated the winners and pinned the rosettes to their bridles. Odette stood calmly whilst the rosettes were fastened to her browband, and Cate felt so proud.

As they left the arena, they were stopped by the photographer to take pictures. Both Cate and Tabby smiled proudly, and Cate was relieved to see Tabby distracted from Bliss's accident.

Afterwards the girls prepared for the fancy dress party. The horses seemed miffed to have their manes and tails sprayed green, and gooey, glittery stuff applied to their coats, but they didn't make too much of a fuss.

Cate was excited about the parade but also a tad worried that Genevieve might drop the flag again. Tabby said she wouldn't dare at the championships – she would be too frightened of the repercussions from Mands.

Inside the arena there were "sea creatures" everywhere. They waited with the other riders from their Pony Club for Mands to give them a signal to begin the parade. They would do the walk and trot circuits first to show off their costumes before pairing off and cantering around.

Genevieve and Gilly were standing in front of them, and they were dressed as sailors in white. Genevieve's outfit fit her to a tee, and her pale blonde hair was left loose, hanging down her back. She had a sailor hat pushed over her helmet and Cate had to admit she looked good. Genevieve and Gilly painted quite a different picture in the same costume, with the curvier Genevieve bursting from her sailor outfit. It seemed to be one or two sizes too small.

"Oh how sweet – you made your costumes yourself?" asked Genevieve airily.

"Of course… and what fun we had doing it!" said Violet jubilantly.

"Ours were custom made by my family tailor," boasted Gilly.

"Congratulations," said Violet. "They fit you *both* so well," with a small laugh.

Mands appeared in front of them, waving her hand and shouting, "We're ready."

They started walking as a group of twenty riders, and Cate could see the seats around the arena brimming with family and friends. As they reached the end of the arena Cate saw Benji sitting close to her parents. She waved joyously at them all.

They began their trot circuit with the riders and horses staying in their pairs. Cate could feel her wig tickling her neck and back and hoped it wouldn't fall off!

After trotting a lap, they halted in the middle of the arena. The first pair of bay horses cantered off with their flags, and it seemed like seconds before they were back giving the flags to the next pair of grey horses.

Genevieve and Gilly were next, and Gilly's small buckskin was dancing around in anticipation. They took the flags from the grey horses' riders and cantered off. They managed to keep side by side this time, with the small buckskin full of excitement, galloping next to Lady's prim canter stride. There was loud music, and Lady seemed to swish her tail tensely to the rhythm of the music.

As Genevieve and Gilly approached, Tabby smiled at Cate and made a thumbs up gesture. Cate smiled back and could feel her adrenalin surging as Genevieve and Gilly cantered towards them. In contrast, Odette was curiously still, probably tired from the weekend's activities.

Genevieve was wearing a stony look of concentration and Cate held out her hand ready to receive the flag. This time Genevieve passed it smoothly to her.

Cate got a firm grip on the flag pole and asked Odette to canter from the walk. Tabby asked Nancy at the same time, and they cantered off.

Odette was suddenly full of herself with energy, cantering almost on the spot at first and snorting loudly. Cate felt a tad anxious that the mare might go out of control and held onto the reins tensely. After a few strides Cate let go of her fears and was exhilarated, feeling the pure energy of Odette's canter and being watched by her family. After circling around, they finished back in the middle, laughing and having the best time, and gave each other high fives.

As they watched the last pairs canter, Cate could see Tabby's Mother sitting with her Mum and Dad. She seemed to be enjoying herself, clapping and cheering along with the other spectators.

When it was time to leave the arena Diane caught up with them outside. Despite her mother looking totally out of place with high heel boots on, Tabby looked happy to see her and asked her if she enjoyed the parade.

"Oh, darling, it was such fun to see you poppets all dressed up. And even the horses! How delightful!" gushed Diane.

"Thanks, Mummy. The weekend hasn't been all fun though," said Tabby as her eyes clouded over.

"What on earth happened, Tabitha?" her mother asked dramatically, opening her green eyes wide and taking a delicate sip from her takeaway coffee.

Tabby confided in her mother, telling her about the accident the day before with Bliss.

Cate and Violet stood nearby waiting for Tabby, not sure if they should stay, but also captivated by the discussion.

"Tabitha, darling, I am sure it will be just fine. You are a gifted equestrian and if Bliss doesn't make it, you will be given another wonderful horse to ride."

"Mother you have no idea how the horse world works. You aren't *just given* amazing horses to ride willy-nilly!" Tabby said fervently.

Tabby took a deep breath and seemed to gather her composure. "Well, the most amazing thing is, Bliss should be just fine," added Tabby firmly.

"Of course... he will be just fine," offered Diane, her perfectly painted lips forming a smile.

"Tabster, it's getting cold. Do you want us to wait for you?" called out Violet as both Cate and Violet huddled with their horses under the awning of the indoor arena, waiting for Tabby.

Diane looked like she was about to choke on her coffee when Violet called Tabby *Tabster,* and Cate resisted a smile.

"I will leave you poppets to get on with your horse things," Diane said in a stiff but not unfriendly voice.

The girls said goodbye to Diane and rode back to the stables. On the way Tabby exasperatedly declared there was no point telling her mum *anything* about horses.

Back at the lorry they packed everything up, with Violet seemingly enjoying the process. Violet bounced around cheerfully, remembering where most things were. She was even able to remind Cate and Tabby where their things were when they stood around looking dazed and confused, tired from participating in such a full weekend.

Around seven o'clock they were ready to leave, and Mum took four weary kids and five equally weary horses home in the lorry. During the journey Cate thought about the weekend and what fun she'd had. She even enjoyed the dressage test – well, mainly the second half – and was thankful to Benji for saving her in her dressage test and teaching her so many new things in a short space of time.

They dropped Nancy and Tabby at Avenley Park and pulled into the drive of Sweetbriars soon afterwards.

Mickey and Pip were sitting beside each other in the stable yard with their fur standing up, braced against the cold, waiting to greet them. Cate realised they must have heard the lorry pull into the drive.

When they jumped out of the lorry, Mickey cocked his ears, barked, and jumped for joy. Pip snaked around Cate's legs meowing and purring happily.

Home sweet home! thought Cate as she gave Pip a cuddle and placed him on his favourite blanket on the ledge in the feed room.

They put the horses in their warm thick beds and gave them full buckets of feed mixed with warm water and molasses. The horses tucked into their supper heartily, and Cate wished Odette a good night and slipped her a sugar cube.

Cate couldn't wait to soak in a hot bath as her feet were freezing! She raced inside the house and greeted her dad with a big hug before bounding upstairs to run a hot bath. Realising she hadn't had time to read her dressage test properly, she took it with her to read whilst she soaked in the bath.

It was a relief to peel her dirty Pony Club clothes from her body. Catching her reflection in the mirror, Cate realised she looked a right mess with her hair disheveled, her cheeks flushed, and molasses smeared across her cheek.

She lowered herself into the warm bubble bath and scrubbed at her face with a flannel. Feeling a little cleaner, she reached for the dressage test she had left on top of the closed toilet seat.

Cate spent the next twenty minutes poring over the judges' comments. At the end of the test the judges said that they were a promising pair with huge potential!

Cate was content and felt a real sense of accomplishment. She was so pleased with Odette and couldn't have agreed with her mum more – that having fun riding was so much more important than winning a dressage test.

She also surprised herself as she began to wonder when she could try her next dressage competition!

Chapter 16

Bliss was not doing well. His wound had become infected and his fetlock was swollen. The vet said he was worried the infection may have spread to the joint. If this happened, there was a chance his leg may never recover, and he could be left permanently lame, or worse yet, the infection could spread further.

Her mum, usually optimistic, told Cate there was a silver lining – the bond that was developing between Tabby and Bliss as she tended to him. But Cate also realised there was a real possibility that they could lose Bliss if the infection spread. If this happened, what would it do to Tabby?

Tabby was at Sweetbriars most days caring for Bliss – changing his bandages, cleaning the wound, and keeping him company while he was on stable-rest. Tabby confessed to Cate that she still felt responsible for his accident, and she felt just awful seeing him cooped up in his stable and hobbling around.

Tabby had given notice to Avenley Park that she would finish riding Nancy by the end of the year. With Bliss out of action she almost changed her mind, but felt she needed a break from riding her bike all over Dalesea to fulfil her commitments.

And she felt better once it was said and done, despite the owner of Avenley Park telling her she wasn't welcome to visit Nancy once she finished riding her.

"And stopped paying!" added Violet, when Tabby told her about the conversation.

The Sullivan family had begun to prepare for the Sweetbriars Christmas Party. Mum had put decorations, including tinsel, fairy lights, and Christmas trees, both inside the house and in the tea room in the stables. Sweetbriars looked inviting and festive in the dark days of winter.

On the morning of the party, Cate helped her mum wrap chocolate and wine as gifts for their clients. Dad put a large sign saying 'Merry Christmas' above the tea room window that overlooked the dressage arena.

Mickey was wearing his new Christmas coat, and the Sullivans had matching Christmas jumpers. Cate's was a deep red colour with white snowflakes falling from the neckline.

Grandma Bea was staying at Sweetbriars over Christmas and helped to prepare the food for the party. Cate was excited that they had a chocolate fondue fountain.

Before the party was due to start, Cate decided to take a handful of carrots to Odette. As Cate walked to Odette's stable, she heard Tabby's voice singing 'Master of the House, Keeper of the Zoo,' from the *Les Miserables* play they were practising at school. Cate paused for a second, enjoying Tabby's sweet voice.

Cate poked her head in to the stable to greet her. "Hi, Tabby. I didn't realise you were here already."

Tabby was applying hoof oil to Bliss's feet. When she saw Cate, she stopped singing and stood up, blushing. Then she smiled.

"Yes, I came early to look after Bliss," said Tabby, as she stroked his glossy black mane.

"He seems jollier today, don't you think? I tried singing to him to cheer him up... or maybe he knows it's Christmas and there's a party on," said Tabby. She giggled as she ran her fingers through his forelock and kissed the side of his face.

"Sure, he looks better," Cate said, trying to sound convincing as she looked into Bliss's dull, vacant eyes. Bliss had developed a poor appetite in the weeks since his injury. He also wore a large bandage from his fetlock to his knee. When he moved, he walked gingerly to get water or to pick at his food.

After talking to Tabby, Cate walked to Odette's stable. As usual, Odette rapped on the stable door with her front leg as if to say *hurry up!*

"Hello, beautiful girl, here are your carrots," said Cate, as she stroked her golden face. "Please don't do anything silly like Bliss, ever. I couldn't bear it," added Cate, giving her a kiss on the nose.

Odette gave Cate a look that said, 'more please,' but Cate had only brought a small handful of carrots as she didn't want Grandma Bea to wonder where they'd gone before the party started! Though she would probably guess.

When Cate returned to the tea room, it was full of people. Tabby was standing with Violet by the log heater. Violet's Mum and Dad were by the window, talking to Mrs. Magill, George, and Grandma Bea. Cate heard George call her grandmother Beatrice, which sounded funny as the family never called her by her full name.

Cate joined Tabby and Violet, and Violet remarked how nice Cate's new hairdo looked without a helmet to hide it.

Cate had blow-dried it the way the hairdresser had shown her in London, and it looked shiny and bouncy.

"Wow! I didn't notice your hair from the stable," added Tabby. "I only have eyes for Bliss when he's around, I'm afraid," she said, giggling. "But I love it. You look sophisticated."

"Yes, it looks fabulous and brings out the green in your eyes!" exclaimed Violet.

Cate laughed and enjoyed the attention for once. She was doing a little spin to show how her hair swished around her ears when she spotted Benji and Adam walking through the door. Adam was holding Elliot the dog, who was asleep, wrapped snugly like a baby in a thick woolen blanket.

Meanwhile, Barry and Owen were at the table, pouring mulled wine into large cups and talking to Dad. Toby was showing Alex something on his phone, and they were both engrossed by whatever it was. Pip was curled up beside the log heater and seemed to be spectating the party with one eye open.

Then the tea room door opened, and Sophia walked in with her mother.

"How lovely of you to join us," said Mum, walking over to welcome them. "I'm Sarah."

In a squeaky girly voice, Sophia's mother introduced herself as Patricia.

"Thank you for having us," said Patricia, as Sophia kissed Mum on the cheek and gave her a small hug. Patricia watched the familiar exchange with a surprised look.

Patricia took off her woolen hat to reveal brilliant glossy red hair, but today it didn't hang past her shoulders, Instead, it was short and in a pageboy style.

"It's a wig," Violet whispered to Cate and Tabby, raising her eyebrows.

Suddenly it made sense, Cate thought, as she remembered the day she'd seen the wigs hanging from the washing line.

"It's definitely a wig," whispered Cate, and went on to explain what she had seen with Beth.

"I like it. I think it's practical to be able to change your hairstyle any which way you like," said Violet matter-of-factly.

"Totally," added Tabby, who often moaned about her fine hair and wished for thicker tresses.

Sophia looked over to Cate and waved, then came towards them, looking relaxed. She was wearing dark blue jeggings with a soft grey woolen top. Her bright red hair fell in natural waves to her shoulders and caught the light reflecting from the log heater. Her black-framed glasses looked more stylish than usual, and Cate wondered if they were a new pair.

"Hello. How are you?" asked Sophia, looking at Cate, Tabby, and Violet with interest.

The three girls replied that they were fine and asked how Sophia was doing.

"Terrific. My stepdad couldn't make it today as he had to work at the shop, thank goodness," Sophia said with a small laugh.

The girls were a little taken aback and not sure what to say.

"Oh, he's not that bad," said Tabby kindly.

Cate and Violet kept quiet and smiled, trying to demonstrate agreement with Tabby.

Sophia replied without hesitation, "Oh yes he is. He's a right pain, and he can be mean and embarrassing. He treats me like a five-year-old."

This was a new Sophia, thought Cate. She wasn't timid or mincing words today.

"Your hair looks fetching that way," added Sophia. "So brave to cut it off."

"Thank you. I wanted a change and it's ever so practical under my helmet. I guess being in London gave me the courage to do it."

"Oh, London! Tell us all the juicy details, you lucky thing," exclaimed Violet.

With all the excitement from the Pony Club Championships they hadn't had time to discuss Cate's trip properly.

"Oh my gosh, it was wonderful! I have the best aunt and uncle, and Olympia was wonderful."

Cate's friends drank in every word as she gave them *all* the details. She also showed them her photos, and the girls joked about how jealous they were.

"Next year, we can go together!" said Cate.

They agreed this was an excellent idea, and even Sophia seemed interested.

"I have some gifts for you," said Violet excitedly, reaching into her bag. She pulled out two small envelopes made of silver paper and gave one to Cate and one to Tabby.

Cate suddenly realised there was nothing for Sophia. She hadn't thought to buy her anything. There wasn't even chocolate as she wasn't a client of Sweetbriars.

"Oh, thank you!" said Tabby, as she slipped a fingernail under the sticky tape to unseal the envelope. Out slid a thin black wristband with a metal horse attached to it. It was painted a mahogany colour with one white leg.

"Oh, how gorgeous." She examined it more closely and declared, "Oh my goodness, it's Bliss! Thank you!"

"Open yours, Cate!" said Violet, grinning.

Cate opened it, expecting something similar. She wasn't wrong – but the horse was a palomino! It was painted a gorgeous caramel colour with a flowing white mane and tail.

"How lovely, it's Odette!" said Cate and she gave Violet a hug.

Cate still felt bad she didn't have anything for Sophia. Luckily, Sophia seemed curious and not awkward, so Cate got on with giving her gifts to Tabby and Violet.

Cate fished the backpacks from below the Christmas tree and handed them over. As Violet and Tabby unwrapped them they seemed pleased, saying they would use them to carry their riding clothes to Sweetbriars.

Tabby gave Violet and Cate woolen headbands lined with fleece in their favourite colours. These were new into the saddlery where Tabby worked.

Then Sophia surprised Cate by pulling out two presents of her own.

"These are for you," she said, pushing the presents into Cate's hands. Now Cate felt even worse and was flustered!

One present was lumpy and wrapped in old-fashioned floral paper. 'Odette' was written directly on the paper in capital letters in a heavy black marker. There was another, softer present, which had 'Cate' written on it, the same way.

"Oh, thank you Sophia – you shouldn't have," Cate said blushing.

Cate opened her present somewhat awkwardly and revealed a chunky woolen scarf. The wool felt smooth to touch, and it was a soft purple.

"I knitted it like the one I gave your mother. I know you like purple, so I hope it's OK," said Sophia as she played with her hair.

Cate was touched by Sophia's gesture. "It's gorgeous, thank you," she replied, as she wrapped the scarf around her neck. With her new haircut, she could feel the softness of the scarf at the back of her neck.

"Well, aren't you full of talents," said Violet in a playful voice, smiling.

Cate's Mum interrupted them, bringing over a wrapped present. "We have something for you too," she said, handing the gift to Sophia.

Sophia's eyes lit up and she beamed as she opened it.

The present was a dark green Christmas jumper – like Cate's, but with a reindeer leaping across the front.

"I'm sorry we didn't knit it ourselves, dear, but we hope you like it anyway."

"I love it. Thank you ever so much," said Sophia enthusiastically.

"Right... I'm going to make a cuppa," Mum said as she surveyed the room. Would you girls like anything?"

The girls were still nursing cups full of hot fondue and they politely declined.

"You should give this to Odette yourself," said Cate, and she handed the lumpy present back to Sophia.

"OK," said Sophia happily. "It's just apple and cinnamon horse bites. I made them myself."

"Wow, you made them yourself? You are a proper little home-maker," said Violet, laughing.

"Well, I try my best," said Sophia, looking at first defiant, and then pleased. Then her face clouded over. "Horses can eat cinnamon, right?"

"I'm sure a little bit of cinnamon will be just fine," said Cate. She hugged Sophia around the waist, hoping she wasn't offended at Violet's joke.

After Sophia went to the stables, Cate told Violet and Tabby she hadn't known her mum had bought a present for Sophia. They all agreed it was great timing, and said how thoughtful Sophia was – even if she was a tad different.

Cate looked out of the tea room window. The weather was dreadful. There was thick sleet on the window and the arena and fields were covered in ice. Cate was grateful to be inside by the log heater.

Cate saw that Elliot was awake and playing with Mickey. They were wagging their tails madly and barking at each other. They circled closer to the log heater where Pip was sleeping, but he didn't want any part of their play. He jumped onto the kitchen bench, knocking a bottle of wine to the floor. The glass shattered, and the room fell silent as people looked towards the mess.

"Oops a daisy! I'm terribly sorry," Adam cried, racing over to scoop up Elliot.

Mum and Dad inspected the mess. "Don't worry, fortunately the bottle was almost empty!" said Dad cheerfully.

Grandma Bea carefully gathered the broken glass and wiped up the spilt wine. She joked that it could have been worse – it could have been the fondue fountain. Adam and Benji laughed and agreed, and Adam put a meek Elliot down and told him to behave himself.

Talk resumed almost instantly, and the dogs sat together quietly by the log heater. Pip had moved to a higher shelf from where he kept an eye on them with his aloof cat expression.

"Oh Pip, don't look all superior and innocent," said Cate as she picked Pip up. He purred loudly and closed his eyes contently.

As Cate cuddled Pip, Benji approached her and touched her arm.

"Now, Cate, when would you like to begin dressage lessons? I hope you're still excited about dressage after the Pony Club Championships," he said jovially.

Cate was thrilled that Benji had brought this up as she'd wanted to ask him herself.

"Well as soon as possible," she said eagerly. "Weekends are good, or after school."

Benji rubbed his chin and said, "I have a spot free on Saturday mornings at ten. Would that work for you?"

"Yes, that would be ideal," replied Cate eagerly.

"OK, then it's set – we'll begin in January."

Benji left them to join Adam, who was talking to Mum and Violet's parents.

Cate grinned excitedly at her friends, pleased at the prospect of beginning lessons in January with Benji.

Then she noticed with amusement that Toby was heaping food onto his plate *again*. But then she noticed something else. Toby dipped the ladle in the mulled wine bowl a couple of times and filled two large cups to the brim. Toby gestured to Alex to take one of the cups, and they high-fived. Then the boys went back to the corner and drank thirstily from the cups. It looked like they were trying to outdrink each other.

It also looked like their parents were watching what was happening. The boys were becoming quite lively. They were rosy-cheeked and giggling at random things on their phones.

Cate told Tabby and Violet what she had seen, and the three girls watched in suspense. Alex and Toby seemed to have not a care in the world, not noticing the attention they were getting.

Their dad approached Alex and led him away to talk. Toby went a darker shade of red as he seemed to realise they'd been found out, and Alex nodded along remorsefully to his father's words.

Alex went back to Toby and shook his head, then threw his cup in the bin. Toby followed Alex's cue, and did the same. They went back to the table somewhat sheepishly and cut themselves large slices of Christmas cake.

At that moment, Tabby's Mum Diane came in. Tabby had mentioned that Diane had hoped to make it for the end of the party and to drive Tabby home for a change.

Diane made quite an entrance. She was wearing a white fur coat that looked like it came from some exotic animal. She took it off to reveal very high-heeled leather boots with black sparkly tights and a sheer, cream silky top. Her blonde hair was pinned up glamorously at the back, with a few loose pieces of hair softly curling around her face. Her make-up looked demure compared to the Pony Club Championship weekend, but she had bright red lipstick.

All eyes went to Diane. Cate and Violet were stunned at how dazzling she looked.

Tabby waved to her mother, who made her way over to them.

"Hello, darling, and you little poppets," said Diane, as if they were all five years old, and she kissed each of them on both cheeks. As Diane leant in, Cate breathed her thick smell of perfume mixed with hairspray.

"Now, Tabitha, darling, I'm not sure if I mentioned that I have a date this evening. That's why I'm a bit dressed up," said Diane.

When Diane said, "a bit dressed up," Violet looked at Cate and raised an eyebrow. Cate rubbed her lips together trying to suppress a grin.

"No, Mummy, you didn't mention it to me. I hope you can you still take me home?" Tabby said, trembling with anger.

"Of course, darling, but we need to leave here by six o'clock. In half an hour. So I can make it on time for supper," she said as she batted her long black eyelashes.

"OK, that's fine, thank you," replied Tabby curtly.

There was an awkward silence, then Violet said bravely, "So is it real – the jacket?" She looked over the exotic fur that was hanging regally from its hook.

Diane looked taken back, "Unfortunately not. But it is very authentic, don't you think?" She laughed nervously.

"Indeed, it looks very luxurious," replied Violet.

Cate and Tabby were stuck on Diane's "Unfortunately not," comment. Tabby looked a bit embarrassed, as they all loved animals.

Diane said she would get a drink and proceeded to the table where she found a glass and filled it generously with red wine.

Sophia had returned from the stables. Now she joined them, asking, "Who's that? Isn't she a tad over-dressed?"

"It's my mother," Tabby said stoutly.

"Wow, for real?" replied Sophia. "She's beautiful."

"Yes, she is," admitted Tabby.

They watched as Diane introduced herself to Benji and Adam, and they seemed to hit it off quickly. Within minutes both Benji and Adam were laughing at whatever Diane was telling them.

A hush fell over the girls as they watched the action of the party winding up. Already daylight was fading and it wasn't quite five o'clock.

Suddenly they were interrupted by Cate's Mum tapping a glass. The room quietened down, and she began to speak.

"Hello, everybody. I wanted to thank you for coming today. It is ever so lovely to have you all here at Sweetbriars at such a festive time of year."

Sarah took a deep breath and smiled broadly at the guests before continuing, "We – our family – feel so privileged to have found Sweetbriars and to have met you all. It's a new beginning for us, which we are thrilled to share with such lovely people."

Sarah took a sip from her glass of wine, then went on to say, "We wish you a splendid Christmas with your loved ones – both your families and four-legged friends. And we look forward to an exciting, and happy new year with you all – our new friends."

People laughed and clapped, then George held his glass in the air and boomed, "And here's a toast – to a very merry Dalesea Christmas, and to new friends."

People raised their glasses to the toast and there was a chorus of "Cheers!" with smiles all around.

Cate joined her family and embraced each one of them warmly. She'd never seen her mum look this happy as she wiped sentimental tears from the corners of her eyes. It made Cate feel so proud of her family and thankful to have them.

It seemed amazing that almost one year ago she'd left behind her old life and everything familiar. Since then, she'd achieved things she never imagined, and discovered that she was more resilient than she knew.

Now she was excited for the new adventures that lay ahead at Sweetbriars!

Ears to Tail Glossary of Horses

Aids The aids are the signals a rider uses to communicate with the horse including legs, seat and hands.
Arena A purpose built area to ride and train a horse in.
Bay A brown coloured horse with a black mane, tail and legs. Bay colours can vary from a regular brown to a reddish mahogany colour.
Bit The metal piece that is fitted in the horse's mouth and attached to the bridle. The rider uses the reins which are connected to the bit to control the horse.
Buckskin A creamy or golden coloured horse with a black mane, tail and legs.
Canter A faster pace than walk and trot and a three-beat pace.
Centre Line The line a dressage rider takes when they enter and exit a dressage arena. It is a straight line going from the letters A to X to C on a dressage arena.
Chestnut A ginger or red coloured horse with a matching mane and tail.

Cob A type of horse that is short-legged, compact and strong. They come in many colours and are usually sweet, gentle and willing horses.

Combination (jump combination) A series of jumps that are jumped in a close series, where the horse takes minimal strides between each fence.

Counter Canter When the outside leg is leading in the canter and the horse is bent to the outside.

Crop or Whip A crop or whip helps the rider control the horse including asking the horse to have more impulsion/energy, go sideways (laterally) or can help with basic obedience training.

Diagonal When a rider changes direction in the arena, cutting it in half diagonally or when a rider rises to the trot, when the outside leg of the horse steps forward.

Dressage The goal of dressage is to create harmony between the rider and the horse as the horse performs various movements in an arena. There are many levels of dressage from beginner level which includes walking, trotting and cantering, to the highest level of Grand Prix with advanced movements such as piaffe, passage or pirouettes, where the rider's aids are almost invisible and the horses look like they are dancing.

Expression A horse that has a flamboyant way of moving could be said to have expression.

Fetlock The joint of a horse's leg at the bottom, above the hoof and in between the cannon bone (or shin).

Forelock The hair that comes out between the horse's ears – the equivalent of a human fringe or bangs!

Forward (same as impulsion) The desire from the horse to move forward with energy when ridden.

Gelding A male horse that is gelded is often easier to control and is similar to a neutered dog.

Girth The strap that keeps the saddle in place and goes around the barrel of the horse, behind the front legs.

Grey A grey horse can be varying shades of grey including white, dark grey, white with dark grey (called dapples) or a fleabitten grey (with dark specks like freckles). Grey horses can change colour throughout their life, fading from a dark grey, becoming whiter and even fleabitten.

Hacking (same as trail riding) Going out in the forest or into nature. It is important for a horse's wellbeing to go hacking regularly.

Half Halt A nearly invisible, simultaneous action of the hands, seat and legs used to capture the horse's attention and regain balance and softness.

Half Passe A lateral movement in which the horse moves forward and sideways at the same time, facing the direction he is going.

Halt When the horse is standing still. A square halt is when the four legs are in the shape of a square and the horse is balanced.

Hands High A metric used to measure a horse in many parts of the world. The horse is measured from the wither (from the base of the mane) and one hand equals four inches. A pony is under 14.2 hands and a horse is over 14.2 hands.

Headcollar (same as a halter) Used to direct and control the horse when leading the horse.

Hindquarters The back part of the horse that joins the barrel - the middle part of the horse.

Jump Types *A Cross rail* fence has two poles diagonally crossed over, with an end of the pole resting in a cup on the wing of the jump and an end resting on the ground. *An upright* has horizontal poles, where both ends rest in the cup on the wings and the jump can have one or more poles. *An Oxer* is a wider jump where the poles have space between them and the horse must jump farther.

Jump Off A jump off is the final stage of a show-jumping competition where the riders that jumped clear in the first part of the competition perform a jump off, where they are judged on time and penalties (hitting a pole) to win a position in a competition.

Jump Wings Often made of metal or wood, are a structure to hold the poles of show-jumps.

Lateral Work When a horse goes sideways and performs movements such as half passe, shoulder-in or leg yielding. Lateral movements can improve the suppleness of the horse and can be wonderful to watch.

Long-side or Short-side of the Arena Refers to different parts of the arena. The long side is simply the longer edge and the short side is the top and bottom of the arena.

Lungeing When a horse is exercised without a rider and circles the rider on a long lead or rope.
Lungeing is useful to get a horse fit, or to let a horse exercise more freely and let off excess energy.
Mane The hair that grows on the horse's neck.
Mare A female horse over the age of three. A female horse under the age of three is a filly.
Mount To hop on the horse.
Noseband The part of the bridle that goes around the horse's nose and is fastened at the throat.
On the bit When the horse arches his neck and raises his back and goes forward softly into the rider's hands. Half-halting helps to get a horse on the bit.
Over-track Usually referred to in walk, when the back legs step over the front hoof prints.
Paces or gaits There are four basic paces which include walk, trot, canter and gallop.
Palomino One of the most beautiful coloured horses, a palomino is gold or caramel with a white mane and tail.
Passage A dance like movement, like a slow trot, with elevated movement of the legs.
Piaffe Similar to a passage but the movement is performed on the spot. One of the most difficult dressage movements to perform and incredible to watch.
Poll The point between the horse's ears.
Plaits The mane is often plaited for horse shows.

Rhythm When training a horse, you should aim for an even rhythm, where the horse is going at a consistent pace.

Saddlecloth The cloth that goes under the saddle, protecting the horse's back, the saddle and absorbing sweat.

Scopey When a horse jumps high, leaving space between the jumping poles and its legs.

Showing (classes) A horse can be showed for its type, breed, conformation or its way of going.

Spooked When a horse gets scared and moves away from something they're scared of. Spooking can be mild where horses simply stop, or some horses will spin and run away, especially young horses.

Stirrup or stirrup iron A rider puts his feet in the stirrup irons, which are connected to the stirrup leathers and the saddle.

Tack The saddle and bridle, also includes other equipment used to ride the horse.

Transition Change of paces e.g. walk to trot, trot to canter.

Trot A two-beat pace in between the walk and canter. The rider can rise to the trot, making it easier to keep in balance in the saddle and a more advanced rider may sit to the trot, making it easier to perform more advanced movements.

Two-point position When a rider stands in the stirrups and takes the weight (seat) out of the saddle. Often used for jumping.

Warmblood There are different types of warm-bloods such as Hanoverian's, Oldenburg's and KPWN (Dutch Warmblood's). These horses have been carefully bred to excel in certain equestrian sports such as dressage and jumping and they often have excellent movement and willing tempera-ments.

Wither The bump at the base of the neck behind the mane and in front of where a saddle is fitted.

This glossary is a mixture of more basic and ad-vanced things to know about horses and riding. Don't worry if you don't understand everything!

If you have any questions, you can contact us via www.sweetbriarsfarm.com

If you would like this series to continue, please leave a review

If you enjoyed this book, it would be much appreciated if you could leave a short review or click the star rating on Amazon or Goodreads. This helps an author more than you could ever imagine!

To learn more about the book series, you can visit sweetbriarsfarm.com and sign up to the newsletter or follow the Facebook page - Sweetbriars Farm Equestrian Book Series. Be the first to find out about all the Sweetbriars news and competitions!

Tabby's Big Year

The second Sweetbriars book, Tabby's Big Year is out now. The book tells Tabby's story including revealing the fate of Bliss! So far, the book has won the 2019 EQUUS Film Festival 'Best Young Adult Fiction,' prize, received great reviews and has also been called a 'must read' from Horse & Hound.

Meet our new cover star – Tyler Russell and her stunning dressage pony, Fairlady at www.sweetbriarsfarm.com.

About the Author

Hollie Anne Marsh is an Australian author who lives in Melbourne with her partner, toddler, and young Warmblood mare Frieda.

Hollie has been riding since she was a little girl, enjoying activities such as Pony Club, show-jumping, eventing, and trail-riding in the great Australian bush.

Hollie lived in England for almost ten years where she had two horses and trained them for dressage.

The Sweetbriars series is inspired by all the special moments Hollie spent with horses – good, bad, funny, and challenging!

Acknowledgements

I am very grateful to have had horses in my life since I was a small girl. They kept me focused throughout my life, spurring me on to finish my studies and develop my professional career so I could afford to own a horse!

I read countless horsey books when I was younger, and I loved a good series where I could get to know the characters and their horses and see how they evolved together.

My hope is that young readers will love this series, and not only will it be fun to read, but it will also inspire and help readers to learn more about horses.

Thanks to everyone who helped make this book better! The early readers who gave me feedback, my editors, my partner for being supportive, and my baby boy for inspiring me and making me smile.

Hollie Anne Marsh
Author of the Sweetbriars Series